Macsen Against
The Jugger

D1453380

NewCon Press Novellas

Set 1: *(Cover art by Chris Moore)*
    The Iron Tactician – Alastair Reynolds
    At the Speed of Light – Simon Morden
    The Enclave – Anne Charnock
    The Memoirist – Neil Williamson

Set 2: *(Cover art by Vincent Sammy)*
    Sherlock Holmes: Case of the Bedevilled Poet – Simon Clark
    Cottingley – Alison Littlewood
    The Body in the Woods – Sarah Lotz
    The Wind – Jay Caselberg

Set 3: The Martian Quartet *(Cover art by Jim Burns)*
    The Martian Job – Jaine Fenn
    Sherlock Holmes: The Martian Simulacra – Eric Brown
    Phosphorous: A Winterstrike Story – Liz Williams
    The Greatest Story Ever Told – Una McCormack

Set 4: Strange Tales *(Cover art by Ben Baldwin)*
    Ghost Frequencies – Gary Gibson
    The Lake Boy – Adam Roberts
    Matryoshka – Ricardo Pinto
    The Land of Somewhere Safe – Hal Duncan

Set 5: The Alien Among Us *(Cover art by Peter Hollinghurst)*
    Morpho – Philip Palmer
    Nomads – Dave Hutchinson
    The Man Who Would be Kling – Adam Roberts
    Macsen Against the Jugger – Simon Morden

Macsen Against
The Jugger

Simon Morden

NEWCON
PRESS

NewCon Press
England

First published in the UK by NewCon Press
41 Wheatsheaf Road, Alconbury Weston, Cambs, PE28 4LF
April 2019

NCP 180 (limited edition hardback)
NCP 181 (softback)

10 9 8 7 6 5 4 3 2 1

ISBN:

978-1-912950-06-5 (hardback)
978-1-912950-07-2 (softback)

Cover art by Peter Hollinghurst
Cover layout by Ian Whates

Minor Editorial meddling by Ian Whates
Book layout by Storm Constantine

"10 x 10 for Judith (10. Not Being the Woodsman of Oz)" by Andrew Philip, first published in *The North End of the Possible* (Salt 2013), and used by kind permission of the author.

One

Macsen scrambled up the rubble bank until he was within reach of the top, then turned himself so that his back was against the broken slope of stone. His hair, his skin, his clothes, his boots, were by now all as dust-grey as his surroundings and, when he was still, he disappeared.

He reached into his bag and felt for his mirror. It still had sharp edges, and his thick, blunt fingers caught against the razor-like shard like a burr snagging the weft of his trews. As he drew it out, he caught sight of himself, and held it there for a moment's literal self-reflection. He had blue eyes, as blue as the midday sky. He checked one, and then the other, and watched the dark pupils expand and contract. Then he tilted the glass and inspected what was over the rise and in the valley below.

A coreship was down by the estuary, feeding. It sat atop a bright pillar of light which pulsed and flickered, but it was so distant that he couldn't hear its signature low, crackly hum. On the far side of the river bank, a slow-moving cloud of rising dust could indicate a tanker, or just a natural collapse of old masonry. He watched as the beige fog rose higher and grew indistinct. Whatever had caused it, had stopped.

He moved the mirror precisely, taking in a view, moving

on. The only real hazard that he could see was a patch of metal blight, down the slope and extending into the river, partially blocking it with debris from upstream caught up in its irregular latticework. There were no signs of other humans in sight, but there were a million places they could hide. Individuals or small groups, he could deal with – they would either avoid him, talk to him, or fight him. It was the larger bands that he was looking out for.

There were no totems, or flags, or other kinds of boundary markers to indicate a hostile tribe, though nothing was without risk: he'd just have to take the chance. He slipped the mirror away, and raised his head over the drift of rubble. The uneven sea of rock revealed itself fully. There were pits and hollows, peaks and ridges, a complicated landscape that appeared frozen, but was treacherous as thin ice. The last of the dust cloud dissipated away to the east. The coreship's luminous meal was like summer lightning.

Macsen kept low and crawled over the top. His sword's crossguard momentarily crowned his silhouette, and then he was down and upright, picking his way carefully through the jumbled banks of loose rock, concentrating on being alert rather than silent. His hands, broad and hard, constantly quested for the best handholds, and his feet, bound tight in their skin boots, flexed and folded to cope with the loose terrain.

His path drew a broken line down to the river, skirting the edge of the blight to do so. The structure caught the scent of the metal he carried, and it strained towards him, creaking as if so many old man's bones. He was too far away, though, to be a strong attractor, and as he pulled away the lattice relaxed with a sigh, sending a little trickle of dust and gravel through the voids.

The water was heavy with brown sediment, soil being washed downstream and away. The muddy flats that extended either side of the river were broad and black: after the constant changes in elevation of the rubble, it would have been a relief to walk out on them. The finely rippled surface shone wetly, unmarked by footprints or tracks. But it would suck and stink, and it held hidden hazards of its own beyond its stench.

The coreship was still down by the coast, a bright fluttering bar connecting it to the ground. He could hear it now, crackling away, making the air jump. There was another sound, too, a more concerted, washing noise, growing louder by the moment. Macsen scrambled quickly back up the riverbank and lay flat on his stomach. The sphere rounded the promontory caused by the blight, churning up the water as it rolled along, half-submerged in the middle of the channel.

The blight had strained at him, but now it quivered and sang. As it burst apart, shards of it, as long as spears and as thick as his thumb, splintered away and hurled themselves out towards the ever-turning sphere. Some fell short with a white splash, but some on a more favourable trajectory struck the exposed hull with a hollow clang and penetrated the outer skin.

As the sphere kept on down the river, the points of entry disappeared and emerged with each rotation. Macsen could count five places where the blight had caught a hold, and he supposed that it was probably sufficient to disable the craft: as the lattice grew both inside and out, the internal mechanisms that kept the sphere going would be corrupted, and the superstructure would ground it on some mudbank somewhere. It might take months, but the sphere would be consumed and converted.

It was strange how that worked. Supposedly the visitors had brought the blight with them, but they seemed either powerless or unwilling to do anything to stop its spread, let alone protect themselves against it. The blight attacked indiscriminately, and, while humans avoided it, they didn't. Or didn't seem to. Ascribing motives and meaning to the machines was problematic.

One splinter had spun away from the main structure, and sat upright in the black tidal mud in front of him. Its severed, exposed end glittered with a rainbow hue which dulled as it healed over. Now it just looked like a strong metal pole. In time, though, it would grow, and eventually coalesce with the main mass.

He needed to move on. He followed the course of the river, with the sphere pulling inexorably ahead of him, until he found the tributary. It ran barely a trickle through the rubble-choked valley, but that was just enough to track, crossing the stream once to climb up on the far bank. At points, the ground was almost bare, with dust-filled shallow depressions scattered over the surface. This had been an open space, in the middle of the city.

The tributary turned at right-angles, and he started to get the sense he was getting close. He checked his bearings, and walked uphill for a short while, staring at his feet. Then he bent down and brushed at the surface. Fragments of red bricks, and the mortar that held them together, made up the majority of the soil. In the distance, the coreship stopped feeding, and the silence was deafening.

The likelihood of the ship passing overhead was low. But he needed to keep an eye on it all the same. Now that the beam had gone, the shape of it partially faded into the haze but was still visible. The four outer cylinders rotated about the central tube as it travelled – no one knew why – and its immensity glided inland. Like the sphere, it followed the river.

The sky grew darker as the coreship slid in front of the sun. Macsen crouched down and wait for it to pass. He didn't need to. They ignored everything that happened on the ground. It probably wasn't even capable of knowing he was there. All the same, there was something almost holy about being in the coreship's presence. Beneath it, the surface of the river tore and fogged, water droplets borne upwards only to fall again as rain in its sky-wake

Where it crossed the land, the rubble stirred. The dust, being the lightest, flew unconstrained, billowing in a smoky column. Smaller pebbles fell as hail, and the biggest boulders growled and cracked against each other, rising and falling, settling into new positions once its influence had lessened.

If the ship had passed directly over him, he would, like the lighter debris, have been raptured toward the sky, then cast down again, unworthy. If he'd managed to hang on to some solid anchor, there was always the danger of being buried under an avalanche of rock. Even the dust could kill, if he let it coat his lungs and clog his throat. Better to avoid it altogether.

After the coreship had gone, the air around him was yellow and tasted of sepulchres. The dust wasn't only old ruins. People had lived here, once, and the ruins were made as much of their remains as it was of tile and flag, brick and stone. Macsen sneezed them out, once, twice, then went hunting for the entrance.

He had to move a rock that hadn't been there before, but it had fortunately broken into three manageable pieces as it rolled down the steps. The way the ground here appeared more flattened made him suspect that there really was a tanker somewhere in the ruins, rolling out the rubble into a compacted pavement of stone. Only for the next coreship, or spike, or jugger, to ruin it again.

He lifted one of the three heavy pieces of masonry aside, and was able to lever the other two out of the way of the door. He squeezed his fingers into the gap between it and the warped frame, and dragged it open with a grating rasp. He took a moment to rest his aching muscles, and drink some water from his tin bottle. The stopper wasn't original: he'd carved this one out of softwood. The bottle was, though, a scratched and dented flask that may have once been painted.

He used his steel, nurturing the scraps of kindling into life in a tenderly, almost husbandly way. The white smoke curled away, up into the clear air, and he quickly caught the flame on his candle-stub. He extinguished the fire again, scattering the burning material and tapping at the embers with his boot. He had a small ceramic disc, with a hole in the middle, into which he fixed the candle. He held it up, and entered the tunnel.

After outside, the darkness was deep and profound, and he waited for his eyes to adjust. There was wreckage on the floor: dust and metal and trailing brittle plastic. The ceiling was cracked and crazed. It might hold for another century, or it might come down tomorrow. Or now, with Macsen underneath it. But with the coreship gone, and no sign of a tanker, it was unlikely.

He stepped slowly, testing each footfall. The candlelight threw startling orange and black shapes across the pitted walls, but he kept his concentration firmly in front of him. Then he came to the main space, cool and still. Somewhere, off in the distance, he could hear a drip, a bright, high sound, and nothing else. It was probably safe to start his search in earnest.

The space was filled with long cabinets, pressed tightly closed against each other. There were gaps into which the carcasses could be rolled, and tracks on the floor to guide them. The nearest gap was filled with rubbish, and the contents of the cabinets either side, mostly gone. A few boards left, but otherwise disintegrated, not even turned to dust. Rather, consumed.

He held the candle up and tried to see if there were markings to help, but all there were were small, empty brackets, in which information had once been displayed. Macsen put his candle on top of one of the cabinets, and spent a while clearing the gap out, shovelling it out into the aisle. The cranks that propelled each cabinet were clotted with age. It was hard work, straining on the ancient mechanism, hoping it would work, praying it wouldn't break.

Eventually, with some cajoling, the cases cracked apart. Inside were books, shelf upon shelf of books. Some would fall apart simply on being touched. Hopefully not the one he'd come for. He checked the titles, and judged that he needed to be three or four cabinets down. Moving the next one was as difficult as moving its predecessor. It seemed so much effort for such a slight volume.

Finally, he was where he needed to be. He retrieved his candle and ran it along the line of titles, calculating where he should stop and look more closely. There. He squatted down in front of the shelf and retrieved the clean skin from his bag, and laid it, fur-side up on the floor next to him. He teased the book out, trying not to transfer dirt to it. The cover was crisp and sharp, and the pages between slightly discoloured: when he opened it cautiously, expecting it to fall apart like snow at his feet, the paper still bent and the words on it were still clear.

He placed the book on the skin, and wrapped it up. The book went in his bag, and his fingers went back onto the ground. There was a hint of vibration, deep and long, and sporadic, so that it was difficult to tell whether it was real or imaginary. He'd learnt to trust his hunches, and knew that underground wasn't where he wanted to be. The racks of books would have to stay open and exposed: he needed to get out.

By the time he picked up his candle, the floor was chattering. As he reached the corridor, the walls were spalling plaster. The door he'd left open had narrowed to a crack, and when he put his shoulder to it, he found that the rocks he'd moved to get in had rolled back. He dug his feet in and heaved. The door shifted, but not enough. He could get his arm through, perhaps his head if he wasn't particular about keeping his ears, but not his broad torso.

The floor buckled under him. If he hadn't been wedged in the doorway, he would have been thrown to his knees. He pushed his hand under the boulder and tried lifting it slightly, while still straining at the door. It edged back. Almost, then, but not quite. The noise was behind him, a deep bass roar of something burrowing up from the depths. A spike. He couldn't have known. It most likely didn't know itself. But he should have made certain of his exit first.

The air thickened. The ceiling was coming down, slab by pre-cast slab. He didn't have long, and he forced himself to make one last push. The door moved again. Enough. Just enough. He threw his bag out, he backed up and unharnessed his scabbard, and threw it after the bag. The slit of light grew hazy, and the sound he coughed up was more of a hoarse bellow. He pushed and gurned and squeezed and huffed.

If the distance between door and frame shrank for any reason, he'd be crushed or cut in half. He had his flailing arms through, and his head and chest. Now it was a matter of pulling his hips and legs after him. If he clenched his teeth, they might shatter with the intense shaking. He felt in the grip of some giant – which, in a way, he was – and powerless.

He dragged himself clear, lifting both legs up and rolling away. There was debris in the air – the spike had broken through, and was flinging rocks like wind-blown blossom. In the depression of the stairwell he was partially protected, and he grabbed hold of both bag and sword before he hunkered down and covered his head with his hands.

It got worse. The noise was deafening. The spike had to be emerging very close by. Loose particles banked up against his curved back in a grey drift, and he could do nothing but shut his eyes and hope. He'd seen people run at this point, panicking, terrified, and get no more than a few paces before being scythed down. He was terrified, but he knew what he had to do to survive.

The storm passed, and the sky lightened. The sound lessened from the continuous roar to a pulsing throb as the spike's rotor slowed. Macsen was stiff with dust, with every pore filled and his skin caked in a film of sweat and filth. He retrieved his water bottle again, and dribbled a stream across his upturned face and nose, snorting and blinking. He took a mouthful, rinsed, spat, and repeated until he could trust himself to breathe again.

The apex of the spike loomed over him. It had come up directly under the vault, not only destroying it, but also everything it contained. It was too much of a coincidence that it had struck while he was there, but that would indicate there was some directing thought behind its movements. Only, and especially only, the juggers showed interest in humans. The spike's rotor finally wound down, and with a pneumatic sigh, ceased its spin.

He dragged himself upright. The dust followed him. Each step he took liberated a tiny cloud of it. Once he was level with the surface again, he looked back at the spike. A huge, narrow cone jutted from the broken ground, which had sunk around its base. It was tilted at an angle, pointing roughly north, but even on a slant, it towered above him. The shell of the spike was grooved and lined by the rock it had bored through. Judging by the number and depth of some of the marks, this was an old one. Perhaps even one of the first ones. They had no distinguishing marks. It was impossible to tell.

He slowly became aware that the sky was filled with loose pages and fragments of paper, all drifting and skipping on the light breeze that was coming in from the sea. All those books, all those words, all lost, bar one. He held out his hands and waited to see if anything would settle on them.

Two

Laylaw waited with the horses. He'd seen the coreship finish up and drift across the beige expanse of rubble, turning the surface over as it went. He'd followed its passage for as long as he could, until its outline was lost in the bluish haze of the horizon. Then he'd been distracted by a sparrow that had sat in the tree above him, eyeing him up, before fluttering to the ground and turning over the fallen leaves by Laylaw's feet, looking for food.

Laylaw still had a bannock in his saddlebags, but knew that if he got up to get it, he'd scare the bird away, possibly forever. So he just sat and watched it, dun and quick, hopping and flicking around the clearing. It seemed to be alone, and he found that strangely sad. A single little bird, on its own, at the edge of the forest, waiting on the arrival of winter: that could be any one of them, really.

After a while, he glanced back down into the valley, and saw another plume of dust rise up abruptly from another part of the ruins. He frowned, got to his feet, and hung his arm around a tree trunk to see how it progressed. If it was a tanker, then he'd expect the source to travel. If it was a spike, then not. The dust rose tall, and voluminous. He wondered if he'd have to ride home alone.

What Macsen was doing didn't make much sense, but then again Laylaw didn't have someone like Hona Loy to order him around. Not that she made Macsen do things, as such. Rather, she inspired him to take these risks. Except he called his journeys 'quests', and her 'my lady', and he seemed content with a smile and a kiss, rather than anything more.

Laylaw wouldn't call Macsen mad to his face. And most of the time, he just did what everyone else did. He hunted, chopped wood, fashioned things with his hands, protected the camp. But those other times, when Hona Loy got that glint in her eye, she'd ask for something that he could neither forage nor make. Macsen had to go questing again, and invariably, Laylaw would be roped in by bonds of filial and tribal duty.

And as Laylaw would have been the first to concede: Macsen was a good man. He was brave and cunning in a fight, a skilled craftsman, a patient stalker, a natural storyteller and a singer of songs. He was handsome and tall, lean and lithe. Laylaw could be jealous of Macsen sometimes. But at others, he would think him an idiot and decide that his own quiet life was simply better.

The dust seemed to be settling. The plume drifted idly across the bare rubble at the same speed as the wind, growing indistinct. Perhaps it was nothing to do with Macsen, and he'd be back soon. Perhaps he was buried under a pile of rubble, and Laylaw would end up spending a fruitless night of waiting, huddled under cloths and skins and cursing his cousin's name, and that of Hona Loy.

When he looked back, the sparrow had gone, and he tutted. He'd liked its uncomplicated company. He took the opportunity to retrieve his bannock – he broke it in half – and sat back down on the soft, piney needles. He made some crumbs and scattered them with a backhanded throw around his outstretched legs. The sparrow didn't fly back immediately, and neither could he see it in the branches above. It might have flown on, back to where it belonged.

Would anyone blame him if he just saddled his horse and rode it and the spare back to camp? He could tell them Macsen hadn't come back, that he'd waited, that the dust plume he'd seen was right where Macsen was supposed to be. It had been, too. Macsen was missing. He was dead. He was too injured to come back to Laylaw, and rather than burden the rest of the tribe with the care of his ruined body, he'd slunk off to die.

No, they wouldn't blame him. They all knew how Macsen was. It was always more of a surprise when he returned, with whatever it was that Hona Loy had dispatched him to retrieve from the ruins, which were dangerous enough without having to factor in the strange, random interventions from the visitors. They'd look at Laylaw, on his own, look at her, frown at her, and turn their backs on her: in a day or two, or a week or two, the matter would be forgiven, if not forgotten. Macsen was a good man, yes, but a stupid one too. He didn't have to go questing. He could have stopped at any time.

And what would Hona Loy do? Would she weep? Would she blame herself for his death? Would she go off into the woods and shout at the trees until she came to some sort of accommodation with what she'd done, and what he'd done? Or would she be silent for a moment, hang her head in remembrance, and then carry on as if Macsen's passing was a matter of little consequence? It was almost worth leaving for the camp now, just to see how she'd react to Laylaw arriving alone.

Macsen knew his own mind, though. There was no hint of coercion on Hona Loy's part, nor lovesickness on Macsen's. It was as if they had independently devised a game, full of nuance and strategy, and then failed to explain to each other the rules. They played, but there was no hope of either of them winning in the conventional sense. The game would only end when one of them wouldn't join in any more.

Laylaw found the whole situation extraordinary. A man's life was at stake, and for what? A token. And to what end? Because he could get it. "Macsen," she would say, "I want you to bring me..." Everyone held their breath, and waited to hear what his next quest would be. When she had spoken her word, and those around the fire had told her plainly that she should stop this nonsense before it got Macsen killed, and told him plainly that he was under no obligation to agree to Hona Loy's request, he would silence them all with his estimation of how long it would take him. Seven days. Five days. Ten days. Twenty days.

Then he would stand up and go and pack, and inevitably, a short while later, while everyone was staring after him, so would Laylaw. Together, they would pack what they needed for the journey, and set out that very moment, whether it was day or night, calm or storm, rain or clear. Laylaw wasn't party to the game, and yet he felt very much a pawn in it. He moved where Macsen wanted him. He waited where Macsen told him to wait.

Who wouldn't resent that sort of treatment? Laylaw tore at the edge of his bannock, and chewed hard, the muscles in his jaw tight and tense under his skin. He was worth more than that, more than simply trailing around after Macsen, wondering if he'd live or die, wondering if they could find their way back to their wandering tribe again. None of the glory rubbed off on him. Everyone wanted to hear of Macsen's latest adventure. No one wanted to hear about how Laylaw – faithful Laylaw, good Laylaw, as if he was a dog – sat and waited.

Perhaps, if he returned alone, he'd have a story to tell at last. How the coreship had gone upstream. How the plume of dust – a spike, yes, probably a spike – had enveloped exactly where Macsen had been heading. How he had waited... No, then: not a very good story at all. They might question him, ask him whether he'd gone down after Macsen, to try and find him, to rescue him and bring him home. Which he wouldn't have done, even though he might say that he had.

This would be the way it would happen: he would ride back into the camp, if he could find it, if it hadn't moved on too far, and they would look up at him, and he would shrug helplessly, and they would frown at him, and purse their lips, and stare into the distance, and that would be that. Words would be superfluous. Everyone knew what might happen. He'd have nothing new to add, nothing they couldn't work out for themselves. The only uncertainty was Hona Loy's response.

In fact, no one would be looking at him at that moment. They'd see him return, leading a riderless horse, and that'd be the last they'd care about Laylaw. They'd all be watching Hona Loy. What did Macsen think he was doing? What was it about her that made him go on these ridiculous journeys? There had to be some hold she had over him, something that happened in the past that she'd reveal otherwise. There was no other explanation.

And yet, there was no bitterness, no shame on Macsen's part, and no cruelty or archness on Hona Loy's. It was true: they treated it like a game. Nothing more than that. Nothing less, either. They both took it seriously. It wasn't as if she was flighty, and made impossible demands one after another. Two, three times a year, that was all. She would ask, and he would give. As if it was the most natural thing in the world.

That left him, Laylaw, here. In the middle of nowhere, looking after two horses, getting cold, getting wet, tired, dirty, scared. Lonely. It was lonely, sitting out after nightfall, while Macsen was who-knew-where. While they were on the journey there, Macsen was quite quiet. Pensive. On the way back, he was his normal easy-going self. More so, even. More himself than usual, if that was possible.

It was the in-between times that were stark. If anything could happen to Macsen, it could also happen to Laylaw, except what happened to Macsen was an adventure, a quest. It was exciting. What happened to the man who held the horses was just fate. What if Macsen came back one day and found nothing, no horses, no Laylaw, not even signs of a struggle? Or that there were signs, blood and trampled ground? Or that a tanker had carved a broad swathe of trees down? Or just Laylaw's lifeless body, face down in the leaf litter?

What would happen? Macsen would accept it as one of those things, and set off on foot, back to the tribe. If he could find the horses, he would. If he could find other horses, he'd take those to replace the ones he'd lost. The ones Laylaw lost. He'd find the tribe, and tell them that Laylaw had gone, with the horses, or that Laylaw was dead, and then they'd want to hear about Macsen's latest quest.

That was it, wasn't it? He was just there to hold the horses. He was interchangeable, disposable, coincidental to Macsen's role. Anyone could stay behind. Only Macsen could go further, complete the quest, come home a hero. He could get swept away by a coreship, or latched onto by a jugger, or more mundanely, attacked by wolves or fall and break his leg: he'd become a mere footnote in Macsen's ongoing story.

Almost as if Macsen were the author of his own tales, and Laylaw just a character in them. A minor character, someone whose name could become corrupted, or forgotten entirely. He only had a part as long as Macsen survived. If Macsen died, then so would he, even if he lived to be a hundred. He would be forever the Man Who Used To Go With Macsen. He'd say his name: "I have a name, you know. Laylaw. My name's Laylaw."

And they would nod and smile, and reply: "That's right. You're the Man Who Used To Go With Macsen." There'd be nothing left to say, except they might add: "Tell me a story about Macsen. One of the good ones." No one would want to hear about Laylaw who waited with the horses, but about

Macsen, who went into the rubble and confronted the dangers there.

There were dangers here, too, in the waiting. There were dangers everywhere. Bandits were dangerous, and bandits only sometimes lived in the cities. Mostly, they hung around the peripheries, exactly where he was. They were lawless, and unpredictable, and intentionally evil. No one could say that about a tanker. Tankers just did what tankers do, and they cared nothing about humans at all.

So, yes. It was dangerous to wait. It was made so by having to wait in one place. If there were bandits, or wolves, or a storm, or a coreship, he could go and hide somewhere until they'd passed. But he'd always have to come back to that spot to meet Macsen. That predictability, that constancy, was what would finish him one day. Maybe not this time. Maybe not the next. But it would, all the same, be the end of him.

He should leave. He should just get up, saddle his horse and leave. Go somewhere an hour away, then set up a temporary camp there. He could ride back in the morning, and see if Macsen had made it. If he had, good. If he hadn't, then Laylaw knew what to do next. Either way, he'd kept himself safe, at a place of his own choosing, and in his own terms.

Except that's not what they'd agreed to. Macsen had said, "I'll see you here later." And he'd replied, "I'll be here." If he wasn't here, Macsen would think that something had happened to him, that he'd been taken, or driven off, or that his courage had failed him and he'd run away. He couldn't imagine what it would be like if he returned to the tribe and told them that Macsen was missing, presumed dead, only for Macsen to walk back in a few days later, ghost-like.

That wasn't true. He could imagine it. It would be awful. Too awful. He'd have to leave, shamed beyond endurance. If he hadn't wanted to come, then he should have just said so. He was as free to refuse Macsen, as Macsen was to refuse

Hona Loy. He could have said no, and he hadn't, and he'd promised to be here when – if – no, when – Macsen came back.

He could say no next time. Then everyone would know where they stood. The others could stare at him as much as they liked. He'd stay seated, and stare right back. Let someone else do the stupid, dangerous thing for a change. He'd done it enough. He'd done it more than enough. He squinted, as if that would help bring back the memories. Fifteen times? Twenty? And when did he start having this exact same conversation with himself? After the third, or the fifth time?

He would say, never again, and the next time, he'd wordlessly sigh, and follow Macsen on whatever quest he was sent on. He would curse himself for doing so. All the way there, and all the way back, but especially when he was on his own. He was as cowardly as Macsen was brave. He did this because he hated himself. He did this because it gave him a reason to hate himself. It justified his self-loathing.

Paradoxically, it made him feel good. If he didn't go with Macsen, then what was he for? He was mediocre at most things, and terrible at some of them. He had a basic level of competence that meant he didn't die, and didn't accidentally kill anyone. Beyond that, he was nothing, a nobody. He was, for all intents and purposes, The Man Who Goes With Macsen. That was his role.

Was that enough? Why wasn't Macsen, The Man Who Chose Laylaw To Go With Him? Because Macsen was the hero of his story, while Laylaw was a bit-player in his own tale. Great things happened around him, but never to him. And actually, that was fine. He'd live longer that way. Macsen would come to grief, and Laylaw would carry on in the strange, uncompromising, unpredictable world he inhabited.

He wasn't angry now. He'd eaten half the bannock, and look, the sparrow was back, hopping around near his feet, hungrily chasing down the crumbs he'd scattered earlier. He watched it dash about on its tiny, wire-thin feet, pecking at the bread with its wedge-shaped beak. Then, as quickly as it had arrived, it vanished.

Laylaw's hand went to his knife, even as he sprang to his feet. It was Macsen. He looked terrible. Like one of the dead. Every part of him was coated in thick white dust, except perhaps his lips, which when they parted, revealed a startling red line. His eyes, though, his eyes were always blue. Laylaw stared at the man's hair, which was stiff and spiked, at his beard that was matted, at his clothes that were caked, at his hands that resembled pale spiders.

"Macsen?" he asked, just to make certain. It was Macsen, of course it was, but for a moment, Laylaw couldn't relate the image of the man in his mind's eye with what stood before him. He was still holding on to his knife, even if he hadn't quite drawn it. Which he should have done. If it wasn't Macsen, and they'd meant him harm, a sheathed knife wouldn't have been of any use.

"I got it," said Macsen. His tight grin broke through the dust. "I got it just in time." He unhooked the bag from over his shoulder and held it out to Laylaw, who took it by the strap and held it away from him. It, too, was filthy. "It's in there. Take it out. Put it in yours. Keep it safe for me." He waited while Laylaw gingerly retrieved the skin-enfolded book, blew on it. "I need to wash," he said. "Wait for me?"

Laylaw found himself nodding. "Yes, of course," he said, automatically. He'd wait, just as he always did. Macsen tapped the sides of his legs, releasing little puffs of trapped dust, and just stood for a little while, looking around, and up at the tree canopy. Laylaw went to stow the book in his saddlebags, and Macsen left the clearing again.

Three

Macsen found a stream. The water was the colour of amber, and cold as a naked night. It flowed down the hill, winding between the rooty bases of the trees, shoring up its banks with rocks. The water flowed along a narrow cut, but he could cup his hands and scoop it up, allowing him to pass his fingers through his hair and rub the dirt out from his pores.

He knelt down beside it, his knees sucking up the moisture from the moss, and thrust his hands into the stream. He watched it turn from gold to grey as the dust loosened and was carried away, and he splashed at it, covering his forearms. He felt the chill heaviness as the water soaked into his sleeves. He used his fingernails on the backs of his hands, then his palms, until they showed pink. He unbuckled his sword, let it clatter to the ground, then pulled his shirt over his head and plunged it down.

The water grew sluggish as it struggled to contain so many particles, more like white paint than forest stream. He used his shirt to scrub his chest, his back, his arms, rinsing and washing and rinsing again. Cold. It was so very cold. He stripped completely, immersing everything, now shivering, his teeth chattering, his skin blue. It hurt. It hurt more than escaping from the spike had. He could barely clench his fists against the pain.

He was done. He was numb, inside and out. No, not done. His bag. He emptied it out, and the contents spilled into the moss, across the green stones and into the water. Oh, he shouldn't have just upended it. He should have been more careful. But the cold, he wasn't thinking straight. He gathered it all up again in his claw-like fingers. No candle. Where was the candle? Back in the vault, extinguished, lost. The candlestick? Gone too.

He pressed the bag down into the stream. He was now shaking so hard he could barely manage to hold it there. The dust in it roiled away, downstream, back to the city which had given it to him. Eventually, they'd all end up there, in the big river, heading towards the ocean, to dissipate and lie undisturbed in the crushing depths. Billions had already made the journey. One more would make no difference.

He struggled to pick up his wet clothes, and his bag, and the things that went into the bag. It took all his concentration, all his willpower. When they'd ask him for his story, they'd ask him what the hardest part had been. Was it steeling himself to enter the ruins? Was it keeping his feet in the rubble? Was it avoiding the blight? Was it locating the vault? Was it finding the right book? Was it forcing his way back out into the day again, with the spike so close?

"Yes," he'd agree: all of those were hard. They were differently hard. They were feats of memory and endurance and courage and knowledge and raw strength. No one asked about this, though. No one ever asked what it was like to come down off that high plateau of emotion. No one ever asked him how that affected him. How it made everything else seem dark and dull by comparison.

Laylaw had set a fire. Macsen could smell it, hear its sharp snap as pine resin popped with the heat. It would be warm, and he would be dry. There'd be something to eat, too. He stood there, bent over slightly, cradling his sodden belongings to his stomach. He couldn't move. Not a step in any direction. Just stood. And shook.

All the dangers he'd faced, all the narrow escapes he'd made. If he did nothing now, how long would it be before Laylaw came to find him? Would he be dead by then? Would he be too far gone to save? Would he stay in that one spot, frozen, a statue, until he crumbled away with time? This was the hardest part, the forcing his way back to reality.

The dozens of little choices he made each day didn't make a story. They were what filled the daylight hours, dawn till dusk, with busyness and drudgery. The quests, though – they were fictions. They had a narrative structure to them that the other life he led didn't, couldn't have. Macsen always wanted to be in the story, and never wanted to leave it even when it was over.

He forced his foot forward. This would not defeat him, though it was getting harder each time. He took another step. It was agony. He was so cold, it was burning. He was walking on needles – not pine needles, actual needles, long and sharp that punctured soles of his feet. He barely had the breath to let out little grunts of effort. Tongues of flame cast shadows that danced around Laylaw's clearing. The man had his back to Macsen, kneeling over, feeding fresh wood to the fire, banking it up until it burned bright and hot.

All Macsen wanted was to be warm again. He dragged each leaden foot another step, another two. He was in the clearing now, and close enough that he could feel the orange light like a kiss on his lips. He dropped what he carried, and let the smoke from the fire wrap around him. A moment later, Laylaw had draped a horse blanket around his shoulders and ushered him closer, pressing a half-round of bannock into his unresponsive hands.

Macsen sat cross-legged, his back covered, his front exposed, his face lifted to the rising sparks and spitting flames.

Behind him, Laylaw gathered the discarded clothes, and draped them over fallen branches all around the fire – his shirt here, his trousers there, his boots upside down and baking. Streamers of white mist spun away as they dried.

Macsen bit into the middle of the broken edge of the bannock. He chewed the mouthful. He swallowed it. He went back for another bite. Laylaw finished hanging up the wet clothes, and cast a few more thick branches onto the fire. A shower of sparks spiralled upwards, and a fresh wave of heat washed Macsen. Laylaw crouched down beside Macsen. "All right?" he asked.

Macsen nodded once, but clearly Laylaw wanted more. "I'm all right," he said. "Spike nearly got me. Came up when I was still in the vault. I was trapped inside." That was too sparse. It wouldn't satisfy anyone. "I had to move some rocks from around the vault's entrance. When I tried to leave, they'd rolled back, blocking the door."

There. Doors were exotic. They were solid, permanent things, attached to standing structures. Tents and temporary shelters didn't have doors – they called them doors, but they were just lengths of cloth stretched across what they still called a doorway. If something had an actual door, then mystery and adventure couldn't be far away.

"You escaped, though?" Laylaw hunkered down further, and turned his head towards him, resting his cheek on one of his knees. Macsen didn't answer straight away, taking another bite of bread. Yes, he'd escaped, otherwise he wouldn't be sitting by the fire, would he? But that wasn't what Laylaw wanted to hear. He wanted to know the margin by which he'd lived.

"By a hair's breadth," said Macsen. That was the traditional measure of escape, wasn't it? No one wanted a story where the teller told of another easy exit, just to the side of the one that was barred. "I had to push my hardest, and even then, it was almost too late. The walls were collapsing, the ceiling coming down. I couldn't squeeze through the gap, until the ground buckled and the door opened just enough. I took off my sword and bag, and made myself as thin as I could. I might have been cut in half at that moment, half-in, half-out, but if I'd stayed I would have been buried alive."

Laylaw was gripped. Macsen could tell by the way his mouth hung slightly open and his eyes grew large and round. "The air was thick with debris. The spike was coming out right behind me, and I had nowhere to go. All I could do was cover my head and hope. The door which had almost trapped me protected me from the worst of it. I couldn't see, I couldn't hear, I could barely breathe. It was like being in the middle of the most monstrous storm imaginable, everything tearing at you with teeth and claws."

"What happened next?" What had happened? Macsen had curled over in the stairwell and hoped to survive. That he had done was due to the spike winding down before it obliterated everything in the area. Hiding was only part of the story if something was trying to find you. The spike wasn't doing that. So how best to tell it?

"I was terrified – no shame in admitting that – and all I wanted to do was run, run as fast as I could away from it. But it was too close. You run from a spike the moment you feel it burrowing beneath you, not when it's already broken the surface. Run then, when it's too late, and you'll get hit by something. So it took all of my courage to stay where I was, with the spike almost within touching distance, just the other side of the door."

Macsen ate more bannock. It was good, and he said so. Laylaw was anxious to get back to the story, but anticipation was part of it. "This travels well," said Macsen. "Excellent flavour. Who made this? Do you know?" He had barely a quarter left, but he held it out in front of him to appreciate it better. The green flecks in it spoke of nettle? Sorrel?

"I don't know. Rey Low? Linell? Does it matter?" Laylaw scowled, and to hide his irritation, got to his feet and broke up some more of the dead wood he'd found. He snapped it with more force than was strictly necessary, and a too-green branch cracked and sprang back against his hand, bruising his knuckles. He gasped and held them, wincing as he flexed his fingers. He threw the wood on the fire, and sat back down, slightly further away than he had been before.

"I just wanted to know who to thank," said Macsen. "The thing about spikes is that you know they'll stop, eventually. What you don't know is if you'll still be alive to see them stop. I cowered – again, no shame in that – under the shadow of the spike as it rose above me. It kept on coming, too. This was one of the big ones, maybe the biggest, scarred and old. Huge. I shook before it. Then I heard its rotor begin to slow. The place where I was crouching was barely big enough for me, and it was falling down around me all the while. Would it hold up long enough? Just. Just."

"There was more dust than air. I had to shake the rubble from my back to stand, and I barely could. I felt pummelled, beaten, exhausted. The spike had come up right where I'd been, right under the vault, and it had thrown up everything that had been inside. The metal and the stone had fallen already, but the paper… The paper was still coming down, like the first snow of winter, in big, fat flakes. You know how it is, you stick your tongue out to catch them. But these weren't made of ice: it was words, and fragments of words, torn from thousands of pages. All gone."

"Except one," said Laylaw. "Except the one you saved." Macsen nodded again. Laylaw wasn't angry with him any more. He'd found the point of the story, the one that Macsen wanted to make. That out of all the contents of the vault, he'd retrieved but one book. And that book was the one that Hona

Loy had asked him for. And because she'd asked him, they had one more book than they had before. The losses were incalculable, so why try to count them? The gains were singular, and so much easier to measure.

"I was filthy," said Macsen. "You saw it. As if the dust of the city had been driven into my skin. And deaf, and battered, and exhausted. I still had to find my way out of the city and back here. Unless you've been down there yourself, in amongst the rubble, you don't know how difficult it is to navigate. It's not like the open country, where there are landmarks. Down there, down in the dirt and the drifts, it's hard. Easy enough to go around in circles, and it's treacherous too: a hole to fall down, and no way up even if you hadn't broken your leg, or buried by an unstable slope."

"And that's without the visitors," said Laylaw, clearly hoping for more. Encounters with visitors were, if not rare, certainly unusual. Macsen had already told him about the spike, and he'd have seen the coreship for himself, floating high above. They'd slipped into the pattern of teller and listener: Laylaw had heard a hundred times what it was like down in the fields of beige rubble.

"There was a sphere, too. Moving downstream on its way to the ocean. I was right down by the river, and I heard it before I saw it. Did I tell you about the blight?" Of course he hadn't. He'd been saving up this part. When he came to tell the rest of the tribe, would he recount the story in chronological order, or would he skip back and forth? Which made a better ending? The blight infecting the sphere, or the paper snow?

"Big growth, half hidden by the rubble, but growing strongly. Even though I gave it a wide berth and wasn't in any real danger, it could smell my sword, and it must have been ready to spore. If you're quiet, you can hear it creak as it bends towards you. But it had better prey today. The sphere came around the bend in the river, and well, I don't know how these things work, whether it has eyes or ears, or whether they work on some other sense and are blind to what we see. It came too close to the blight, which just burst apart. Great harpoons of metal flew out, some falling short, but many hit their mark with a boom like striking a hollow log."

"Now, it didn't break the sphere apart, and didn't sink it, but each time it turned after that I could see the spears in its skin, and I swear it was turning slower when it went out of sight. It'll be consumed soon enough. If the sphere makes it to a beach somewhere, that'll be where the new blight will be. Otherwise, it'll sink to the bottom of the sea, and good riddance to it."

No, his encounter with the spike and its aftermath was a good end. The first time he'd tell it – Laylaw didn't count – he'd give it all the flourishes and then slowly bring the book out of his bag, and on bended knee, raise it up. Hona Loy would enter the circle of firelight, her face flushed with heat and embarrassment, and take it from him.

She'd hold it wrapped for a while, then she'd peel the skin away from its cover. Despite everyone watching her, she'd have a private moment with the book. She'd look at the title, and perhaps even raise it to her face to sniff that old-book smell. Then she'd open it carefully and read a few tentative words, at first silently, then at the urging of others, aloud.

That would be the end of Macsen's part. He would retreat to the edge of the circle, and she would hold everyone's attention, declaiming someone else's considered phrases in her low sing-song voice. He'd listen, he'd close his eyes, he'd dream of another age where they had so many books, no one person could ever read them all.

"Macsen?" asked Laylaw. "Are you sure you're all right?" The other man had crouched right down in front of him, and was resting a hand on his blanket-shrouded shoulder. In the other, he had Macsen's water flask, proffering its heavy, cold contents.

Macsen wiped his tears away with the back of his hand, and took the water, though he didn't drink any at first. He knew what Laylaw thought of him: that he was mad, and dangerous, and selfish, and probably lots of other things besides, but that was enough to be going on with. That Laylaw resented being dragged around after Macsen, simply because they were cousins.

That one day, Laylaw was going to have to go back to the tribe and tell Hona Loy that Macsen was missing in the rubble, presumed dead. Because that would be how it would happen. There'd be no body, no division of his personal property: an empty pyre, if they bothered with that part, and nothing else. They might retell some of his most daring quests. They might drink a toast to him, and cast the dregs into the heart of the fire.

They might carry on telling his stories. They might even make up new ones about him. Macsen against the tribe of giants. Macsen against the wolves. Macsen against the jugger. Macsen rides the coreship. He'd be a legend, a myth not just for his tribe, but for all of the tribes. His name would live, even while the person was forgotten.

Had he done enough for that yet, or did he need to do more? One last blinding feat, while he still could, that would keep them talking forever. It was up to Hona Loy, he supposed. He raised the water to his lips and felt the cold flood his mouth and chill his throat. "I'm all right," he said. He looked carefully at Laylaw, studying his shadowed eyes and his furrowed brows. "Thank you. Thank you for waiting for me."

Laylaw edged away. "You should get some sleep," he said. He rose and kicked a few of the half-burnt logs back into the fire. They recaught with a roar, and a wash of heat fluttered over Macsen's face. Everything was again in stasis, and Macsen, like the story he was going to tell, could be put to bed. He rested the water on the ground in front of him, and half-rolled, half-fell onto his side, so that he could still see the fire.

He lay, warm and wrapped, watching the golden fronds of flame sprout and wither. Jets of white smoke hissed out as the resin boiled, and the snap and crack of trapped gas sounded too loud in the clearing. Sparks ascended to join the cold stars above, while the shadowed shape of Laylaw squatted nearby. While he kept watch, Macsen slept.

Four

They broke camp in the morning, using the embers of the previous night's fire to bake some damper. It was burnt on the outside, undercooked in the middle, and tasted of wind-blown ash. Neither man complained, nor particularly enjoyed it. It was all they had, and this close to the rubble the pickings were slim. For whatever reason, plants found the old sites barren ground.

Each man had a shaggy-haired horse to saddle, and though their feet were halfway to the ground when mounted, it was better than walking. The horses may have disagreed, but their opinions were never sought. With bags slung fore and aft – the precious book just behind Macsen's right thigh – they left the clearing after raking the fire out, the last of the smoke mingling with the faint morning mist.

They headed north, through the forest and across the river. The last vestiges of tumbledown walls barely broke their stride. The works of man had subsided back into the earth, and instead they saw deer and auroch, rabbit and marten, kite and crow. They found the steep-sided valley and rode up to its head, towards the hollow they called Craig Low.

It was one of the places their tribe visited, especially at this time of year, to catch the last of the summer grazing on the tops. Sometimes they went elsewhere – Black Bay, when the fish ran, or Long Loch, to pick the fruit, but more often Craig Low was their last stop in the highlands before turning south to escape the hard bite of winter.

The look-out posted by the deep pool, where the route upward narrowed to a point, leaned down from her tree. Her ridged ram's horn swung about her neck as she dangled, and she spoke through berry-stained lips. "Did you get it, Macsen? Did you get it?" No pretence, no obliqueness from the girl. She wanted to know, and now.

Macsen squinted up into the branches. "Is that you, Kay Lee? I've been away so long, I barely recognised you. Your hair has grown a full yard, and your legs another foot." He winked at her. "So, now that you have three feet, you'll be needing another shoe."

"Macsen, stop teasing me and tell me." She laughed. "Will there be a story tonight?" She lost her grip on the branch and tumbled out onto the path in a clatter of twigs and leaves. Macsen was off his horse in a single leap, his hands fluttering around the girl, clearing the debris from her face and checking the look of her eye.

"That'll learn me," she said. She pulled a face, and let Macsen lift her to a sitting position. "You won't tell anyone, will you, Macsen? The shame of it. I don't want to be known as someone who can't keep their place." She spat out some lichen, and put the back of her scratched hand across her mouth.

"There'll be a story tonight," said Macsen. "And Kay Lee falling from a tree won't be part of it, I promise you." He pressed his palm to his chest. "They won't hear of this from me, I swear, if you get back up there and keep proper watch. It's important that you do, yes?" He raised her to her feet and set her down again, touching his fingers down in amongst her crown of golden hair.

"Yes, Macsen," she said, eyes momentarily downcast. But before she turned back to the tree trunk she had to scale, she looked up at him. "Can I see it? While it's still day? Can you read me something from it? Just a few words?" Can I be Hona Loy, if only for a moment? Can I pretend that I sent you on your quest, and not her?

Laylaw, ignored and superfluous, blurted out: "No! No, you can't. You can wait like everyone else." Like me. You can wait like me. I've not seen it. I've not looked inside it. Macsen's not offered to read so much as a word of it to me, and I went with him to the edge of the rubble and waited for him, not knowing whether he'd come back.

Kay Lee shrank back, half-hiding behind the tree. Her bright, grubby face became mask-like, uncertain as to what emotion she was feeling. Macsen rose from the ground and frowned at Laylaw, as he stared defiantly back. But only for a moment, because Laylaw broke and looked away. It was true, though: that was the shameful part of it. He was jealous, and that... that could kill.

That was enough. He'd refuse the next quest. Let Macsen take someone else. Let them wait. Let them wonder. Let them be the one who came back alone and told Hona Loy that Macsen was lost. Perhaps – and he hadn't considered it before – Macsen wouldn't go without Laylaw. And he could beg and plead and cajole and bully as much as he liked. Laylaw wouldn't do this again. Not if it meant turning into this, a sharp-tongued coward.

"I'm sorry," he said. "Too little sleep and too much awake." Which was also true: while Macsen had slept uninterrupted, he'd had one eye open all night, watching the dark wood and the star-pricked sky for shadows, and one ear cocked for noises, both natural and unnatural. Otherwise, wolves could take their horses, and a coreship have them hanging feet above the tree tops, before they'd known anything.

"Forgive him, Kay. You'll get to hear everything tonight — how I sneaked through the rubble, dodged the visitors, found the treasure and barely escaped with my life." As he spoke, he mimed each part. He tiptoed through the city, crouched and darted around the machines, delved into the ground for the book, then shuddered with imaginary impacts before springing up joyous and resurrected.

Macsen's clowning, rather than Laylaw's gruff apology, turned Kay Lee. "Waiting's so difficult," she said. She looked up at the tree she had to climb. "Don't you dare start without me, Macsen. I don't want to miss a thing, not a single word." She casually reached up a brown-skinned arm and hooked her hand over the lowest branch. She pulled, and her feet pressed against the rough back. She scaled the trunk quickly and easily, and her clothes merged with the overlapping leaves until she was hidden. "You hear me? Not a single word."

"I hear you, Kay Lee," called Macsen, shaking his head in wonder. Laylaw had to suppose that was for his benefit: surely Macsen had to know that his stories were prized, to be shown off and admired. Otherwise, what would be the point of risking his neck, and Laylaw's, if not for something special? "Come on, Laylaw. We're almost home."

Macsen meant the tribe, not the tents and temporary structures. The tribe was permanent. Where the tribe was at any given time depended on the seasons, and the movements of other tribes. The tribe was home, high or low, north or south, forest or meadow. It was Laylaw's deepest fear, that one day they'd move on without telling him where they'd gone, while he and Macsen were off questing.

Macsen would be able to find them again, following the trail that would be obvious to him: a hundred or so people, all their animals, all their belongings, trampling down the vegetation with their feet and hooves. Obvious to Macsen, not so to Laylaw, who couldn't see the nose on his face without it being pointed out to him.

He wouldn't have to worry about that any more, as he was never going off with Macsen again. He'd stay with the tribe, and not have to worry about his skills – or lack of them – as a navigator and tracker. The tribe was always going to be in sight from now on. That was another reason, not that he needed one, for not going questing.

And yes, his motives came down to fear and jealousy and selfishness. None of them were laudable. They were nothing he could voice in public or private. Yet he felt them all deeply. He was adamant now. No one could force him to admit to his reasons. His no would be no, and it would be his final answer.

They turned the corner, climbing up the final rise, and there was Craig Low, a bowl of land with a lake at the bottom. The rock rose around it like a rough grey curtain, which draped into the water at its lowest hem. Water that Laylaw knew to be cold and black and crystalline. The tribe's tents were pitched between the edge of the lake and the point where the river began its headlong tumble into the valley.

The greens and browns and creams were all he'd ever known. The wooden frames and the cloth that covered it, the lashed-together structures with boughs and bracken roofs. The sum total of his experiences had been lived out in and around the smoking fires and hurdles, along the foot-worn paths that turned rapidly to either mud or dust, sleeping next to other people as they turned and snorted and snored.

In considering that it was all he'd ever known, he thought for a moment about how his ancestors had lived, separate, in their own brick boxes, atomised, alone. The visitors had destroyed that way of life utterly. If the tribe tried to put down roots, they'd be dug up again. They now kept moving because the visitors moved too, on their unpredictable, ever-shifting patterns.

The moment that Macsen appeared, he was mobbed.

People crowded around him and escorted him into the camp. They pushed Laylaw aside in their hurry to touch some part of Macsen, to tug at his sleeve, to pat his back, to grasp his hand. Soon, Macsen was well ahead, pressed in on every side, propelled forward, and somehow, Laylaw was left leading not just one horse, but two. He couldn't remember taking the reins of Macsen's mount, but he must have done.

He stopped, and watched, as the knot travelled on, weaving around the tent posts on the way to the central space. Laylaw listened to their excited voices, and saw the way they were bright and alive with joy and anticipation. He turned away, a horse on his left and his right, to tie them to a hurdle. He realised that Macsen had left the book in his saddlebag.

Had he realised, or was he too busy receiving the adulation from the crowd? At some point, he'd remember, but he wouldn't come back for it himself – he'd send someone else to collect it. Or would he? There was a question of trust. Who would carry the precious gift to him, so that he could give it to Hona Loy?

Laylaw, of course. Macsen had left it with him deliberately, knowing that his cousin would carry it safely, and not give in to the temptation of peeking inside, even just for a moment. He growled at his lot, and opened the flap of the bag, feeling inside for the skin wrapper. There was nothing. It was empty. Macsen must have it after all.

He started on the tack for his own horse – not his horse, but the tribe's – and laboriously untying the loops and binds on the mostly metal-free harness, when he felt a touch on his hip. He turned and looked around, then down. A child started up at him with grey eyes. "Laylaw, Macsen says bring the book."

Laylaw squinted down – Myco, that was the boy's name. "Tell Macsen he already has his book," he said, and went back to dragging the saddle off of the horse's broad back. He struggled, not with the weight of it, but with its ungainliness, and set it on the ground as quickly as he could. The child was still hovering, uncertain as to what to do, hopping between two contradicting orders.

"Laylaw, Macsen wants his book," he said. And Laylaw was about to tell the boy again that Macsen had to have the book already, because it wasn't where it ought to have been, when he thought that perhaps he'd not checked properly after all. He brushed his hands free of horse hair, setting it free to drift on the wind like thistledown, and had another look.

He first checked the same bag, then all the bags hanging from Macsen's saddle. Then he did it again. "It's not there," said Laylaw to the boy. "You saw me. Every bag. Macsen has to have it. Go and tell him it's not here." Still the child was reluctant to leave, and Laylaw had to shoo him away. "Go. Go and tell him."

Laylaw frowned as the boy first walked, then ran, back to Macsen. There was no reason for this strange cruelty. Macsen had the book. He'd had charge of the book the whole time, except for when he'd given it to Laylaw while he'd been washing. That wasn't quite right though, was it? Laylaw had had it the whole night, and had given it back in the morning.

And neither was that. Laylaw had packed the saddlebags. He'd put the book in the bag on the right, and he'd fastened it too. Macsen had asked him where the book was, and Laylaw had told him exactly where. Had either of them checked before they'd left the clearing? Had Macsen simply taken it on trust? What if Laylaw had made a mistake, and the book had fallen out?

It was impossible. It hadn't fallen out, and yet it couldn't be found. Laylaw felt the first flush of panicked sweat wash over him. What if he'd got the horses mixed up? That was it. That was the answer. The book would be right where he'd put it, in the front-right pouch of his own saddlebags. His saddle was on the ground, and he knelt down next to it. His hands were shaking as they flew to the straps, making opening them difficult.

Behind him, he could hear Macsen and the rest of the tribe – it would have been almost everyone by now – getting closer. Their feet, their voices, their confusion. There had been a quest, and Macsen had ridden out. He'd told them he'd been successful, and yet where was Hona Loy's gift? Was Macsen lying? Was he playing with them? Which was it?

Laylaw had to find the book quickly, but he'd barely got the flap open by the time they all arrived. Before anyone could say anything at all, he thrust his hand inside. Nothing. There was nothing there. His fingers explored every crevice, but it wasn't a big pouch, and it didn't take long. His heart began beating in slow, heavy thumps.

"Laylaw?" said Macsen. "Laylaw, where's the book? You said you'd put it on my saddle?" The bags creaked and rustled as he looked for himself. All of his usual paraphernalia was there, Laylaw knew, but not the book, which Laylaw also knew. It gave him a few extra moments in which to check the rest of his own saddle. The book wasn't there. It wasn't on either saddle.

Everything was now shaking, even his voice. He swallowed against his dust-dry throat and tried to unstick his tongue from the roof of his mouth. "I don't know. I can't explain it," he said. "I put the book right where I said I put it. Didn't you check it? Didn't you look for yourself, to make sure?" If he was finding it difficult to look at Macsen, he could barely take his eyes off Hona Loy.

She stared at him, and he at her. She'd always had such large, luminous eyes, set beneath perfect brows and either side of a thin, delicate nose, and above pale, defined cheekbones. Her chin was small, slightly pointed like that of a cat, and pink lips that turned readily to a white-toothed smile. She wasn't smiling now, though. She was so, so disappointed, and it was worse than Macsen's anger.

"I'm sorry," he said to her. "I'm sorry. I don't know what's happened. I can't explain it. I put it in Macsen's saddlebags. I put it there, I swear, and now it's nowhere to be found. It... I... I don't know!" Everyone was going to blame him for the disappearance – or non-appearance – of the book. Yet it wasn't his fault. He'd done everything right, from the moment Macsen had asked him to look after it.

Macsen had walked around his horse to search the bags on the other side. He stood facing Laylaw, his fingers clenching and unclenching. "If you give it to me now, we'll say no more about it," he said. "But this is no longer a joke. You know I nearly died retrieving that book, the closest I've ever been to death. Just... hand it over from wherever you've hidden it."

Hona Loy was still visible over Macsen's shoulder, but Laylaw was being confronted directly, and he had to deal with that, rather than plead his case to her. He looked for a moment at his feet, and then looked up. Macsen was flushed, and bristling with indignation. "I gave the book to you, Macsen. I didn't lose it," said Laylaw, just before the fist connected with the side of his head.

He went down, more startled than hurt – not that it didn't hurt – and in the short time it took him to recover, Macsen was being dragged back, his arms clutched, his puffing chest encircled. Laylaw put a hand to his ear, where the blow had connected. His skin there was hot, almost burning to the touch. He got to his feet. "You lost it, Macsen. You lost it."

Macsen struggled to free himself, to launch another, more sustained attack on Laylaw. Laylaw knew he'd lose. He was smaller, weaker, and less capable than Macsen. But he also knew that he was telling the truth about what he'd done with the book. That gave him courage, because if he spoke the truth, right was on his side and he'd win the fight, somehow.

Macsen disappeared into the forest of arms, sucked into the crowd and moved away, resisting all the while. He was left on his own, except for Hona Loy. And the horses. She was desperately sad, and she believed it to be entirely his fault. She didn't need to articulate that, he knew it anyway. Then it was just him and the horses. He watched her go, but couldn't call after her. He'd said everything already.

Five

Early in the morning, while the sky was still dark and Craig Low wreathed in mist, Macsen came to find Laylaw in the single men's lodge. He shook him awake, not roughly, but not gently either, and waited outside while his cousin picked his way through the sleeping bodies to the entrance. He emerged, face slack and skin pale, and walked loose-limbed and stumbling away from Macsen and towards the lake.

Macsen followed in Laylaw's footsteps until they both stood on the wet shingle shore, neither one looking at the other. Above them, the stars were winking out as dawn encroached, but they made no sound and even the wind was still. It was cool, perhaps the last day of the year when it wasn't actually cold at that hour, and Laylaw was apparently in no hurry for Macsen to explain himself.

"We need to go out again," said Macsen. His voice seemed unnaturally loud in the silence. "We need to go out again and find the book." He ground the toe of his boot into the grit, listening to it rasp and cover the soft sound of Laylaw's breathing. "You'll come with me, won't you?"

Laylaw snorted, and a few moments later, Macsen could see him shake his head slowly. "Why would I want to do that? The truth is I gave you the book, and you lost it. But because you can't admit to that, everyone now thinks I'm a liar or a thief. Then you hit me. In front of them all. So why don't you tell me why I should go with you?"

"We always go out together. Always. Whatever happened to the book, we need to find it, and we need to find it together. That's how it works, Laylaw. It'll be somewhere between here and the clearing – probably it's still in the clearing – so it won't be difficult. Just ride out, pick it up, come back. That's all. Say you'll come." Macsen tried not to show he was rattled by Laylaw's initial refusal, which had never happened before.

"If it's going to be that simple, go on your own and find it. You don't want me there, making a mess of things, do you? According to you, I can't even put a book in a bag, or worse, that I deliberately don't put a book in a bag to spite you." Laylaw looked over the lake, with its low, lazy ripples, and he ducked down to fetch a small shard of spalled slate.

"I never said you lost the book deliberately. I never said that." But they both knew that no one blamed Macsen, and everyone blamed Laylaw. "I don't know how the book came to be lost. I gave it to you, and you say you put it in my saddlebags. If that's what you say you did, then that's what you did."

"And it wouldn't have killed you to tell everyone that, would it? They think I've ruined the quest, sabotaged it for one reason or other. They wanted their story, Macsen, and now they hate me." He flicked his wrist and let fly with the stone, sending it skimming across the surface of the lake. It bounced four times in quick succession, and then the black water swallowed it up.

"They don't hate you. They just want you to make it better. They still want their story, and when we find the book – when you find the book – then everything will be forgiven, and forgotten. That's why we need to go and do this. To save your reputation. To make things right again." Macsen watched the last of the stone-ripples subside and waited.

"My reputation?" Laylaw growled at him. "If you were worried about that, then why didn't you defend me at the time? You could have said, 'It's not Laylaw's fault. It's mine.' But you didn't. You kept your mouth shut and let your fists to the talking instead. I don't know what happened to the book after I put it in your saddlebag. Do you?"

"If I knew, I'd have the book, wouldn't I? But I don't. I don't have the book, and I did have the book because I gave it to you. So we have to go out and find it again, don't we? It's not like I'm asking you to go into the rubble. I'm not asking you to fight bandits and I'm not asking you to fight wolves. It's a day's journey, two at most. It needs to be found before it rains. Before winter comes. Before we move on. It's the gathering soon."

Laylaw scooped up another stone and tossed it from one hand to his other, back and forth. "I don't want to go out with you again. I don't want to go out with you ever again. I'm done with that. I'm done with you. Do you understand that?" He threw the stone, less successfully and with less control. Three clear bounces, and a slide.

"Don't you see? You have to help me find the book. Not because I think you lost it, but because the rest of the tribe think you lost it. They'll remember that. You could live to be a hundred, and you'll still be that person. Listen to me, Laylaw: you have to join me, or there'll be no life for you here."

"I'm listening, cousin. You could still tell them all that you made a mistake. That none of the blame is mine. You can own your own mistake, your own carelessness, and not put it on to me." Laylaw snorted. "But you won't do that, will you? You'd rather they think I'm worse than nothing than have them think you're less than perfect."

"That's not true," said Macsen. He couldn't look Laylaw in the eye, though. He ran his tongue over his teeth and bit at his lip. "I was angry. I thought I had the book, and I didn't, and you were the only other person who could have lost it. Perhaps I didn't think before I acted. What's done's done, though. We need to work together now, to mend what's broken."

"You broke it. You broke it: not me. And you could fix it, but you won't. And the only reason you need me now is to keep your lie going. You think I've not got a choice now, but I still don't want to go with you. Out there is scary. Out there, just the two of us, and the wolves and bandits and juggers and coreships and spikes and who knows what else. I'm afraid. Then you leave me! You leave me on my own and I have no idea if you're coming back or not. If you want the book that you lost, then find it yourself."

"I need you with me, Laylaw. It won't be the same. We've always gone together. Right from the very start, we've always gone together. I get this feeling that if you weren't there, waiting for me, I wouldn't come back. Just as long as I've someone to come back to, I know it'll be fine."

"You can't even apologise, can you? You can't say sorry for doing this terrible thing to me. Even before this, I'd decided that I wasn't going to go on any more quests. I decided it was just too dangerous for me. I never wanted to be a hero like you, and I didn't have to be. Now this: all the people I have ever known, will ever know, think I either stole the book, or deliberately hid it from you."

"I'll make it right again." Macsen ventured to rest his hand on Laylaw's shoulder. The first time, he was shrugged away, but the second time, he wasn't rejected. "What we need is a story, some reason why the book's missing. Going away and finding it again will give us time to –" He hesitated and scrubbed at his face with his fingers. "Time to make something up."

"Make something up?" Laylaw stepped sharply away. "Make it up? You don't have to make anything up. Just tell them you lost the book. Tell them you lost the book, and that you're going to find it again. Take someone with you if you want. Take them all. Just not me. I'm not going with you."

"It needs to be you, Laylaw. It can't be anyone else. We work together so well. We're blood." Macsen could see he was failing, and he had to try something else. "What about Hona Loy? I can't let her down. And neither can you."

Laylaw twisted around and checked behind him, making sure she wasn't standing there before he spoke. He moved closer, and lowered his voice. "Leave her out of this. This has nothing to do with her. This is between you and me, and why you're blaming me for losing the book."

"I've seen the way you look at her. I've seen the way you look away when she notices you. She's keen on you, Laylaw. You could have asked her if she'd step out with you at the gathering. You could have. Not now. Not unless we get the book back. You and me, yes, of course it's you and me, but not just you and me and it never was."

"It always felt like just you and me." Laylaw shivered. "Out there, away from the tribe, in the wilderness, walking the edge of the rubble, listening for the wolves, watching the skies for coreships, feeling the ground for spikes, wondering if a jugger was hunting us, or whether we were about to walk into a trap set by bandits. Just you, and me."

"It wasn't like that. It was never like that," Macsen said. "They were all with us. Hona Loy was with us. The whole tribe was with us. We were carrying them with us, all the time. Every step of the way. They went with me into the rubble. They came back with me when I returned. They never left us, not for a moment."

"They were never with me, though, were they? They were with you. I don't come in anywhere. I don't turn up in any of your stories, except at the start and the end. I don't matter. You matter, but not me. You do the quests, not me. You're the hero, not me. You tell the stories. Not me. Hona Loy barely knows I exist, anyway."

"Then make her know. Come with me, and we'll find the book together, and we'll bring it back together, and we'll both be heroes. You'll be part of the story, and you'll get to talk with Hona Loy. Come on, Laylaw. You're part of the story already. We can't leave it like this, can we?"

"You'll put me in the story? Properly? You'll tell them that it wasn't me that lost the book. That, I don't know, the book was just lost, and we had to go and find it again. You'll tell them that, before we leave?" Laylaw had been dragged around, from obstinate determination to wavering agreement. Macsen felt relief like cold rain. It wouldn't be the same without Laylaw, his talisman, his keepsake.

"I won't say anything about who lost the book. I'll tell everyone that the quest is incomplete, and we need to go back out and see that it's done properly. Stand by my side as I make the announcement. They'll look and they'll see Macsen and Laylaw together. It'll be fine, cousin. It'll be better than fine: Hona Loy will be there, and she'll see you and me, and she'll know that we're a team, each one relying on the other, yes?"

"One last time, then," said Laylaw. "One last time." His shoulders sagged and he stared across the lake at the rocky cliff on the far side. "I'll sort out the horses, get everything ready. By the time I'm done, most people will be up, and you can tell them then. This is it, though. This is the very last time. I'm not doing this ever again. If you want to carry on questing after this, you'll have to find someone else. Do you understand?"

"I understand. Thank you, Laylaw. I'll get my kit, and I'll meet you in the centre." He said he understood, but he didn't. Why wouldn't anyone want to go on quests, and come back with stories? It was the best thing in the world – the only thing in the world left to them that mattered. They couldn't build cities or leave monuments any more. All they had were stories.

Laylaw walked away, slowly. Perhaps he was wondering how he'd agreed to something he'd been so adamantly against. Macsen didn't wonder. He was good with words, and words gave him power over other people's feelings. He knew he'd be able to talk his cousin around, and look, there was Laylaw, going to saddle the horses again and ride out with him.

Macsen wasn't ready to give up the quest, and he wasn't going to give up questing either. And whatever Laylaw said now, he knew that the next time Hona Loy stood up in front of the central fire and called out his name, Laylaw would end up following him out into the wilderness. He waited for Laylaw to fade into the morning mist, then headed back into the collection of tents and shelters.

Those who'd already stirred greeted him, but he was now in a hurry. He needed to collect everything together, and get to Laylaw before his cousin changed his mind. A few bolstering comments and everything would be right: assure him of his place in the story, of his prominence in the tale to come, and a stirring speech to the assembled group, then off again. Out, down the hill, across the valley, and back into the forest to continue his adventures.

He slept in a different shelter to Laylaw – still a single man's lodge, but higher status – and quietly gathered his belongings: his sword, his knife, cloak, bag. He upended his bag onto his blanket to check that everything was still there. He knew he'd lost the candlestick along with the candle, but he wouldn't need it this time. He wasn't going underground.

When the skin-wrapped book fell out, he stared at it for a moment, before covering it with a corner of the blanket. He lifted it again, just to check he wasn't seeing things, but no: it was definitely the book, and it had definitely been in his bag. His stomach contracted to a tight knot of anxiety. He looked to his left and his right. Each sleeper had his back to him. He carefully but quickly put the book back in his bag, and sat back on his heels.

He picked up his water bottle and uncorked it, swilling the last of the contents. His hand was trembling as he refastened the stopper. Laylaw had put it in there. He'd forgotten he'd done that, and Macsen hadn't checked. Or had he himself transferred the book from the saddlebag into his own satchel? He swallowed. The water was cold going down.

There was no way he could admit to having the book now, and save face. Not after all the fuss that'd been caused, and certainly not after the argument with Laylaw. They'd have to ride out anyway, and Macsen would have to confess he'd already found the book, and that they were making their journey just for show.

That wouldn't work either. Laylaw was bound to be furious with him, to a degree where he'd be liable to say something, to someone. Not that anyone would particularly believe him, and certainly not over Macsen, but his cousin would harbour a lingering grudge against him. Those were dangerous where everyone had to rely on everyone else to keep them safe. He didn't want that, for his own sake, and for Laylaw's.

Laylaw wasn't a bad person. Quite the opposite. Macsen liked Laylaw: he was dependable and quiet and shy and lacked imagination. Macsen wasn't lying when he said he needed Laylaw. He needed someone exactly like Laylaw in order for him to go questing. If he told Laylaw he'd had the book all along, there'd be no chance at all of them riding out together again. As it was, Macsen thought that Laylaw was malleable, and he'd fold again under pressure.

There was nothing for it, then. Macsen would have to conceal the book and, at an opportune time, pretend to find it. He could do that without any difficulty: all he would have to do was wait for Laylaw to be somewhere else and simply produce the book and tell him he'd found it. Laylaw would never know.

And if there was a chance for embellishing the story, he'd

take it. Perhaps Macsen could find some evidence not that the book was missing and had been found in an entirely mundane scenario, but that it had been spirited away from him somehow, and then discovered in mysterious circumstances. Circumstances which he'd be at a loss to explain, but that would add a supernatural tinge to his story. What if the book itself was haunted, possessed by one of their long-dead ancestors? Or the author himself?

That was even better. Vengeful spirits would be a new angle in his tales, one he'd never used before. He packed the rest of his equipment in his bag and slung it across his shoulder, then carried everything else out into the cool, damp day. They'd be back by nightfall. There was absolutely nothing to worry about.

Six

"Shouldn't we be retracing our steps by foot?" asked Laylaw. "The skin you wrapped the book in isn't going to be obvious. We could ride right past it and never know."

He peered into the undergrowth either side of his horse, but couldn't fix his eyes on any part of the ground for long enough to even tell one plant from another.

Ahead of him, Macsen waved down his objection. "The best place to look for the book is where we lost it. And the most likely place where we lost it was back in the clearing. It'll be somewhere there. If we can't find it, then we work our way back. But I'm sure once we check the clearing, we'll find it soon enough."

"But what if we go past it in the light, and by the time we get back to that spot, it's dark? That's no way to search for something, is it?" Laylaw stared at the ground again. He soon gave up. "Are you sure about this, because I'm not. We should look everywhere we can, while we can. We can't even be certain of our route. We can only guess at it."

"We'll find it. If we go back to the clearing, make a good search – while it's still light – then we'll save ourselves a whole day when we find it there. If we spend our time lifting up every leaf and blade of grass, it'll be dark long before we get there, and we'll have to camp out again. There and back, Laylaw. It's simple enough." Macsen dug his heels in and stretched out the distance between him and Laylaw, and made it impossible for Laylaw to carry on remonstrating.

They rode on in silence after that, down the wooded valley and away from Craig Low. They crossed the flood plain and forded the river without incident, unless waiting for a coreship to go by counted. It seemed to follow a west-east chord, which made it the second to head in that direction in as many days.

The spinning cylinders dragged up a cloud of forest debris. Not just leaf litter and fallen branches, but whole trunks and tenuously-rooted plants, and suddenly above the swaying, straining tree-tops, one, two, three deer, flailing and bleating as they were hoisted into the dun-coloured air. The coreship moved on, off towards the rising sun, and on the trailing edge of its influence, everything that was up came down.

The deer plummeted to the ground, out of sight. The fall would kill them or cripple them, and if there were wolves following the coreship's progress, they'd eat well. Laylaw thought of hot, roast venison, and then about facing hungry wolves, and then, inexplicably, about Hona Loy. The juxtaposition of images made him shiver.

Macsen watched the coreship slide out of sight, the sound of its passage no less than that of a giant's creaking limbs. Then he rode on. It seemed to Laylaw that his cousin was even more pensive than usual for the journey out. Possibly because he'd already completed his quest once, and was now faced with doing so again.

It hadn't seemed that way this morning. Macsen had been eager, enthusiastic even. It might just be the coreship. They were frightening, and this encounter was the closest the Laylaw had ever come to one. Normally they were distant things, and he'd only ever seen the harrowed ground they'd passed over long after they'd gone. This was immediate and threatening. If they'd been in the forest themselves, they might not have even spotted it before it was too late. They and their horses could have ended up like the deer: broken-backed and wolf-food.

Macsen reached the tree-line, and ducked down under a branch. A little while later, so did Laylaw. It was green and dark under the canopy, still with the trickle of litter pattering down after the coreship had deposited it higher. The wind blew, and the trees bent, and grit and brown needles dropped on their shoulders and into their hair.

If the book at been under the coreship's path, it'd be gone forever. They'd have to be extraordinarily lucky to find it. And even if it wasn't directly underneath, the downwash of debris was such that it'd be buried by now. Macsen's horse stopped at the strip of disturbed ground, and wouldn't go on. He dismounted and waited for Laylaw.

It didn't look that different, but to them the signs were obvious. The undergrowth struggling through a thick carpet of freshly-turned leaf mold. The fallen branches scattered in strange, propped-up piles, the stones like soft pillows, the fresh, earthy scent of digging. The strip was very new, and still settling, covering pits and obstacles alike. Laylaw dismounted too, and, taking his horse by the bridle, led it out.

It was difficult. The ground underfoot was unreliable. They had to pick their way, high-stepping, coaxing their mounts, through the debris field, and it took what felt like forever. Once they were across, Laylaw sat down for a rest, only to be stared at by Macsen.

"We can't stop. We have to press on, before it gets dark. I know you're tired, and the horses are tired. I'm tired too, but we can't stay here. The deer. It's too dangerous. We've horses, and you know wolves prefer their meat red." Macsen swung himself into his saddle and looked down at Laylaw. "You know I'm right. We need to get to the clearing as soon as we can."

Laylaw sighed and stood. He patted his horse on his shaggy-maned neck, and checked each of its four legs, making sure it hadn't come to any harm. They would, of course, have to cross the strip on the way back too, and it wouldn't be much better then. "You don't know the book's there. It could be out here. It could be anywhere."

"We'll find it. It'll be there. Trust me, it'll be there." Macsen's mount was reluctant to start off, but he dug his heels in hard and flicked its hindquarters with the flat of his hand. It started to plod away, and Laylaw was left with no option but to follow. Except that he did have an option, but he hadn't exercised it when he had the chance, and now... not now.

He climbed up and nudged the horse into a walk. The clearing ought to be another hour away, over the ridge and facing the rubble. But he was now certain that they'd lost their original track, having had a chunk of it erased by the coreship. Whether they could pick it up again remained to be seen. Without doing so, they'd have an impossible task. Yet Macsen remained confident.

Laylaw remembered all the other times when he'd been out with Macsen. Hona Loy had set the quest, and his cousin had just assumed that he could complete it, without question. Without planning, even. Laylaw wouldn't ever have done that, and never would in the future. Was that the difference between them, then? That Laylaw would consider the problems first, and Macsen would meet them head-on, solving them as he found them?

That he'd lived as long as he had was therefore something of a miracle, and that he was, and always had been, on borrowed time. It suddenly struck Laylaw that Macsen wasn't looking for the book, or for any of the other trinkets demanded by Hona Loy. He was looking for death. And not just any death: a heroic death, in an age where death was a matter-of-fact occurrence and usually as a result of an accident.

Macsen would keep on questing until he died. Laylaw was necessary in all of this, because he was the one who'd have to go back to the tribe and tell Macsen's final, and glorious, story. And if Laylaw didn't ride out with Macsen, Macsen couldn't quest. He was going to be, whether he liked it or not, whether he'd been asked or not, responsible for Macsen's death.

Had he known this all along, and had simply blocked it out? Or had the realisation been creeping after him for a while and had only just now ambushed him with the truth? He watched Macsen's back. Sometimes – twice at least in his memory – people sneaked away from the tribe and killed themselves. Once by hanging, once by drowning. In that case, there wasn't even a body. They were just swept out to sea, and never seen again.

There'd been just enough ambiguity there to pretend it had been accidental. But the person concerned, a young man obsessed with the visitors and what they'd taken away, was deeply troubled. No one else was surprised when he'd abandoned his foraging basket and walked into the churning waves. It hadn't been the weather for swimming. The water was numbingly cold. Apparently, it hadn't taken long before he stopped moving.

Was that Macsen? Was he wresting one artefact at a time back from the visitors, and always doomed never to pull back enough to banish them from the world? Was he hoping that one day he'd have the excuse to just sit down and make it all stop? It was never going to get better. They were never going to defeat the visitors. They had sticks and stones, a few iron weapons. If humanity had been able to drive the visitors away, they would have done so when things like powder guns and flying machines and rockets existed.

There had, so the stories went, been huge battles that laid waste to whole cities. In those stories, individual visitors had been destroyed, but there were always more to replace them.

After a while, man's ability to make bullets and bombs became so eroded that it didn't really matter any more. Billions died. Their bones were ground up under the weight of tankers and then scattered by coreships.

Macsen wanted to make new stories. Stories about good things. Stories about man outwitting the visitors and winning through. Except that he couldn't make those stories have a happy ending. The visitors were always going to be with them. They were always just over the horizon, waiting for them to put down roots and settle.

No one would be able to build a house again with the expectation that they could live in it. Die in it, yes, when the rafters came down and walls fell in. But not live. Not raise children there. Not plant crops around it and tend them. Not have their graves marked, even. Nothing permanent, except the stories they told each other.

Macsen's story would end, and they would have those stories for as long as they told them. But that it would end, and end with his defeat, not his victory; that was for certain. Laylaw felt a degree of sympathy for him, but he was determined not to join him on his search for immortality. He was going to make it back to the tribe, book or no book, Macsen or no Macsen.

For all the ruined dreams of what had gone before, Laylaw liked the simplicity of his existence, the shared struggle, the sense of belonging that he had now. Let Macsen wish that the visitors had never come and never stayed. To Laylaw, they were part of the landscape, no worse or more alien than wolves.

They crested the ridge, more or less side by side, a few trees apart. The down slope seemed strangely bright, and as they picked their way through the forest, they could see why. Shattered fragments of white wood lay over the undergrowth, and the air was rich with the scent of resin. No coreship had caused this. A tanker, perhaps the same one that Macsen had supposed was in the rubble, had rolled through, smashing and crushing everything in its path.

Stumps had been pressed into the ground by its vast weight, and the trees themselves snapped off at the base and flattened into the soft earth. Branches flailed like broken wings across the cleared path. It was recent. Last night, or earlier today, while they were still on the far side of the valley. Laylaw couldn't hear it now, so no later than that.

He pulled a face and dismounted, tying his horse's reins to one of the upstanding trees before approaching the clear-cut swathe. The contours of the ground had changed with the passage of the tanker, going from gently undulating to squashed flat, with only the underlying rock supplying any shape to the land at all.

He imagined it moving through, a giant roller, as tall as the trees, the chevron-shaped markings on its outside edge biting hard into the ground, spears of metal extending and retracting as it turned, and the roller slowly but inexorably flattening everything in the way. The splintering and cracking of wood. The pops and sighs as the pressure was released again. The terrible noise rising to a crescendo, then fading away.

"Where was the clearing?" he asked. He knew. Or at least, he thought he knew. "Was it here?" It might be impossible to find again, but the fire-ash might have survived as a dirty, smeared-out stain on the flattened ground. They could orient themselves from that. What good that would do remained to be seen. If either of them had dropped the book here, it was lost.

Macsen gazed out over the tangle of broken trees. "We can still do this," he said. He shuffled out into the swathe, checking his footfall carefully. "You try that way. I'll go this. Tell me if you recognise anything." Macsen gestured off to his left and started picking his way over the half-submerged logs, pausing at every step to plan his next move.

Laylaw called after him. "Are you mad? Are you actually mad, and I've not realised until now? We'll never find the book now. It's gone. It's over. You can't win every time, and this is one of those times. There's no shame in admitting defeat, that the visitors and the world and life have beaten you. It happens. It happens to everyone. Let's go home, Macsen. Let's go back to where we belong."

Macsen carried on threading his way through the toppled lumber. "It's here. I know it's here. I just need to find it." He stopped and looked around, then headed off in a different direction, diagonally across the cut, towards the trees on the far side. Laylaw didn't follow him. Instead, he went back to their horses. Macsen's was tethered a little away from Laylaw's, so he brought them together and sat down next to them.

He waited for a while, long enough for the sun to struggle out from behind the sheet of grey, rain-threatening clouds and send down shafts of weak, watery light. Then he heard Macsen calling him. He got up stiffly and walked to the edge of the trampled swathe to look for him. Macsen was in the distance, holding something up in his hand intermittently as he traversed the hazards.

It looked like the book. It looked like it, yet if Macsen had actually found it, he'd be the luckiest person alive. The clearing had been obliterated, anything they'd left in it pressed into the ground by a weight so mighty that it altered the contours of the land. Laylaw blinked and squinted. The thing that Macsen had did indeed look like the skin-wrapped book.

It was impossible. Yet there it was. Macsen had an incredible ending to his story, and he'd never stop questing now. He'd go on and on, trying to replicate this moment, and it would be terrible and wonderful for all those around him, and he wouldn't care if they lived or died, just as long as the story was served.

Macsen was grinning. Of course he was. He would ride back a hero. And Laylaw would be the doubter, the one who never believed and was proved dramatically wrong. He still had no idea how Macsen had pulled this off, but the evidence was there all the same. Time to play his part one last time, then. He clapped, and the sound of his applause was strange and hollow in the clear air.

Seven

It had been so simple. Get away from Laylaw, make a perfunctory search of the clearing, come up with the book, act surprised, and head home. The tanker had ruined that. There was nothing else he could do but carry on with the plan, and hope that Laylaw wasn't going to question him too closely. It looked like a miracle, pulling the book from the wreckage. Miracles were, by their nature, impossible to explain. Yet explain it he must.

"It was just there," he said. "It was just there, right by the very edge of the track. Another foot's length closer and it'd be buried with the rest of the clearing." He held it up in both hands. "We must be the most fortunate people on the whole of this island. To have found this twice over. We've done it. You and me, cousin."

He studied Laylaw's face for any trace of scepticism or doubt. Yes, there was a certain sardonic cynicism about him, but also a weary acceptance that Macsen's charmed life seemed to extend to even this. Laylaw had seen Macsen come back from his quests victorious every time. Why should now be any different?

It was different because he'd manufactured the ending for the first time. The Macsen he wanted to be had somehow become subsumed by the Macsen that he wanted everyone else to see. He'd crossed a line with this deception. He knew it. He knew it in his soul. He knew that even if he lived an exemplary life from now on, this moment would always haunt him, for as long as he had conscious thought.

He could confess. He could tell Laylaw exactly what had happened. How he'd found the book in his satchel, and decided there and then to cover it up just to save his own reputation, and damn Laylaw's. Out here, the two of them, cousins. They could work something out. There could be reconciliation and forgiveness. They were blood.

The words died on his lips. Instead, he grinned more broadly and let out a hearty chuckle. "No one's going to believe this. It's a good thing I have you here as a witness, Laylaw. It's a very good thing. So what are we waiting for? Let's get back and share this good news. There's going to be a story tonight, such a telling that they'll talk about this forever."

Laylaw's expression had frozen. He was no longer looking at Macsen, but behind him. Macsen's peripheral vision gave him no clue. He'd have to turn eventually, so why not now? He glanced over one shoulder, and caught sight of the edge of it. He knew what it was. He knew what it meant.

The jugger was the same as all the other juggers. A scuffed egg, pointed tip facing downward, floating at just over head-height, trailing whip-like tentacles whose tips flicked and twitched against the broken branches and desiccating needles. Its mouthparts were blades, not yet spinning. But there was a deep brown stain around them which spoke of a great many victims.

But which one of them had it fixated on. Was it him? Or was it Laylaw? He went to stand next to Laylaw, and they looked at the jugger together. It seemed content to wait while they sorted themselves out. Small pieces of debris drifted up underneath it. Individual needles. Moss and lichen. Beetles.

"You go back into the forest," said Macsen. "I'll go over the other side again." He wanted to give either of them the best chance of being able to lead the jugger away from the other. That was how juggers worked. One at a time. Seemingly with no memory except for the one person who was their designated prey. Macsen moved quickly, as quickly as he could, crossing the swathe and into the trees again.

The jugger was still waiting. Macsen could just about see Laylaw, hanging off the back of a tree trunk, peering around it, arms half wrapped around it, as if it might protect him. It wouldn't. Not from the jugger. Nothing would, not time nor distance. A jugger didn't sleep, didn't stop, not once it had chosen. When it had killed, it was a blank slate, drifting without purpose until it saw someone else. Then it remembered what it was made to do.

Macsen stopped. Laylaw was thinking it, so why shouldn't he? Which of them would he want to be picked? He didn't want to die. He wanted to carry on, making stories, telling tales, having adventures. But he'd seen what he was becoming. He'd already compromised himself. He put other people at risk.

Why not now, why not go out on a high point? Macsen against the jugger. Leave the book here for Laylaw to retrieve, and run, down the hill and away from his cousin, drawing the jugger after him and leading it a merry dance until it finally caught up with him, exhausted, with barely enough strength to spit on its stained casing. Do that, then. Redeem himself.

He filled his lungs. "Come on, then. Come on. Choose me. Chase me. Leave him alone and come after me." It wouldn't make any difference. If it had already chosen Laylaw, then there was no persuading it otherwise. If it had already chosen him, then Laylaw would be able to report that those were his last words. Brave words, foolhardy words, caring words.

"What are you waiting for? It's me you want. I'm the one you've been after all along. I'm the one who hates you. I'm the one who cheats you. I'm the one who steals things out from under your noses. Me. Macsen." He slapped his chest and bellowed his defiance. "Me. I'm your enemy. Take me, not him."

The jugger started to slip across the bare strip towards him. Had it chosen him? Or was this just some random movement? Then it started to speed up, though they never reached any more than walking pace for almost all of the hunt. The jugger was now between him and his horse. It would easily cut him off if he tried to reach it. Macsen placed the book down, propping it against the bole of a tree. "Take the book back, Laylaw. Make sure you do."

Laylaw's only contribution was to shout, "Run. Just run." Macsen raised his hand – this was goodbye, and they'd never see each other again – and he started to jog downhill, towards the treeline. He needn't check that the jugger was following him, because that's what juggers did. All the same, he paused, and looked behind, and yes, the jugger was weaving through the trees, just as he had moments before.

It didn't really matter how fast he went. He could sprint off, and the jugger wouldn't respond. He could walk just ahead of it, and the jugger wouldn't care. At some point, he would have to stop. He'd need to sleep. The jugger wouldn't. If Macsen could get far enough ahead, he might snatch a few hours rest. All the time, though, the jugger would be closing the distance.

If it caught him, the tendrils dragging from its central mass would lash out and stun him. Then the spinning blades would cut him to bloody ribbons. If it caught him? When it caught him. There was no question of if. Macsen against the jugger could only end one possible way. It was his job, his last duty, to lead the jugger away from Laylaw, and away from the tribe, and die in as a remote location as possible.

It was the most, and the least, he could do. It might be

months until it found another human to fixate on. From here, the most desolate location was back into the rubble. He already knew there were no tribes there, and no bandits either. Nothing but dust, broken stone and machines. And the blight.

The blight was interesting. He'd already seen it throw itself at a sphere, puncturing its outside, lodging deep within and presumably sending its shoots out to devour its innards. If it did that for a sphere, which was huge and represented a clear target, would it do it for a jugger, which was much smaller, and held much less attraction?

The blight he'd found down by the river had been ripe. His sword alone had made it quiver. But then the sphere had come along, and all the explosive tension in the structure had been expended. It had been two days since, not long enough for the same stress to build up. If, however, it had only been the bankside part of the blight that had thrown itself at the sphere, might the landside half still retain some of that power?

He didn't know. However, the result of Macsen against the jugger seemed a little less certain. His one break was knowing where to find a patch of blight. If he could get himself to it, and divest himself of all his metal, and crawl right up to it, and then somehow avoid the shrapnel when it felt the jugger close in, and it managed to instantly disable the jugger sufficiently to stop it moving – something it had singularly failed to do with the sphere – then he could still die in a dozen different ways, but not be killed by that particular jugger. He would have cheated not just death, but fate itself. He'd have an even better story than the one about the book.

He'd never go back to his tribe if he did survive. He owed Laylaw that much, not to drag him out into the wilderness and get him killed. This time had been too close: half the time, the jugger would have gone for Laylaw, and it'd be his cousin waving a miserable farewell, never to be seen again. No, if he lived through this, he'd strike out on his own, head south, join another tribe, and tell the stories he'd collected as if they were about someone else.

He'd need a new name. He'd use Macsen for the hero of his tales. But they wouldn't be about him. Then it struck him: Laylaw. He'd call himself Laylaw. Laylaw would narrate the quests that Macsen went on, because wherever Macsen went, Laylaw went too. Yes, there'd be two Laylaws, though they'd never meet. It all made sense. This was Laylaw's way out. This was what he'd wanted. To have a quiet life, and perhaps start a family. He'd become Laylaw.

After all, it was Macsen who quested, and after this, Macsen would be dead. Laylaw would certainly say that there was no chance of Macsen ever coming back from the jugger. Even if the blight did infect the jugger, the chances were that Macsen would still die, either from blight-shards, or from the damaged jugger. It'd be a noble end to a brilliant story: Macsen tricking one visitor to destroy another, and falling at the last moment.

If, once the blight had done its work, he could take up his sword again, strike the jugger, drive the point through its exposed innards, twisting and probing like his was exploring a man's guts. The tentacles might still be active – he could hack at them like the fabled hydra, and go down fighting. Perhaps he would go down fighting. Perhaps his thin sliver of an idea wouldn't work out. Perhaps he was always going to die today.

He kept up a good pace, widening the distance between him and the jugger. He'd need that space to navigate properly in the rubble, and position himself close to the blight. He broke through the tree line, and headed directly across the debatable land between the forest and the city, where scrubby weeds hauled themselves up through the broken pavement of brick and concrete.

The rubble, greys and browns, stretched out ahead, in drifts and waves and dunes. Only fleetingly was there any pattern: the hint of a building, the shadow of a road, some underground space still somehow intact. He'd normally pause and check for bandits. He didn't have time. The jugger cleared the trees and unhurriedly came towards him. Macsen climbed up on the first mound of rubble tall enough to give him a view, and he scouted ahead, looking for that bend in the river where the blight grew.

He couldn't see much, but from the rise of the land on the other side of the valley, he could tell roughly where to head. Getting to the river itself would allow him to sight along it. Then it was just a question of staying in front. After this, it was going to be difficult for him to keep sight of the jugger – so he took one last look, then skipped down the slope.

The rubble wasn't made for quick movement. He had to climb, he had to scrabble, he had to divert and back up and try again. His progress slowed, and he began to sweat. Either he was going to make it, or he wasn't. He had to start taking risks: more risks than usual. If he slipped and injured something, or brought an unstable slope down on himself, then that would be it. But so would being caught by the jugger.

Then abruptly, he was by the river, and below him were three people, as muted and beige as he was himself. They were as startled as he was, and they raised their weapons at him. One had a bow, and an arrow already nocked. Macsen managed to check his momentum and not tumble down at their feet. "Jugger," he said. "Jugger."

Now, if they believed him and still killed him, it was likely that the jugger would also take one of them. Was it worth the risk, if they still wanted the things he carried? Evidently not, as their expressions went through surprise, to greed, and finally to fear. "Keep away from us. You hear? Keep away." They ran to the west, along the broad river bank, towards the sea. As quickly as the encounter had started, it had ended. Macsen against the jugger. It was always going to be just him and it.

The kink in the river was to the east. If he squinted, he could make out the rectilinear extrusion of the blight as it jutted out into the water. And the jugger appeared just over the next rise, before disappearing again behind a rubble pile. It was close. Was it too close? He jumped down to the river's edge, where the mud smoothed out the rock, and ran along it. The jugger, sensing his change in direction, was probably moving parallel to him, higher up the bank, unseen.

He was leading it straight towards the blight. He could see it properly now, the sharp spears of metal in a jagged framework. The river-facing side was incomplete: far too soon for it to have repaired itself. The other side, though. He was counting on the rest of it being primed to spore. At some point in this ridiculous race, he was going to have to ditch every last piece of metal he was carrying. Sooner, rather than later, and still while at a run.

His bag – that had his bottle, and his flint and steel – went over his shoulder and onto the ground behind him. His knife was on his belt, and his belt had a metal buckle. He'd take that off last, because he needed to shrug off his sword's harness first. The straps that held it tight to him were difficult. He slowed slightly, and had to look down to see what he was doing. His fingers felt thick and unresponsive, his breathing started to go ragged.

Ahead, the blight felt him. It creaked. He undid the main strap, paused just long enough to drop the harness to his knees and step out over it. The jugger was coming. The belt: he still had the belt to undo. The blight shifted again, starting to build up the stress that would propel shards of sharp metal through him.

He managed the clasp. His belt dropped to the ground and, with the waistband of his trews held up in his fist, he stumbled up to the blight and tried to climb the bank to reach where he needed to be. Where was the jugger? It couldn't be so close, because the blight would have exploded. It wasn't so far away though, that it wasn't pressing itself into new, lethal shapes. He dug his feet in, and one-handed, beached himself on top of the first rise.

There was the jugger, directly opposite, blindly unaware of anything except him. The whole of the blight was singing with anticipation, and he was too close to it. He was going to get hit by the spores. He slid back, grinding his front against the sharp rock, tearing his shirt, scraping his face. The sound from the lattice reached final, high-pitched, perfect note, and then disintegrated.

Eight

Laylaw watched Macsen go. He watched the jugger glide after him, the hazy cloud underneath changing as it left the swathe crushed by the tanker. It passed close enough to the book to lift it slightly, then deposit it back down on the undergrowth with a slight slap. The skin cover flapped open, and lay still.

When he was sure they'd both gone, he crossed the tanker-path and picked up the book. Partially unwrapped as it was, it allowed him his first glimpse of the cover. Of another world. Of machine-printed words, of manufactured paper, of cuts and binding. Feeling stupid, he lifted it to his nose and sniffed. It smelt of age, of dust, of memories.

He used his rough fingers to open the boards. The endpapers were a deep blood-red crimson, startling against the bone-white of the pages. His thumb brushed against the edges and the skin caught at a random point. He cracked the stiff paper, and inside was black writing, small and neat, arranged in ordered lines of similar length and spacing.

He knew this was a book of poetry: that's what Hona Loy had asked for. Laylaw couldn't read more than a few words, but there were those amongst them who were literate. As a last and lasting gift, she couldn't have chosen better. It was, however, now going to be him that presented it to her. The thought made his stomach squirm as if he'd swallowed a live fish.

He'd always found it difficult to talk to her. Macsen hadn't. Macsen had never found it difficult to talk to anyone. Macsen had never found it difficult to talk. It was a gift he had, and he'd had so many of them: he was brave, strong, capable, learned, sociable, a hunter, a crafter, a story teller. People went to him for advice. They wanted him on their hunts. They sat next to him at the fireside. And now he was gone.

He wasn't coming back. It was impossible that he could. No matter what Macsen did, he couldn't escape the jugger. No one ever had, so it was a safe assumption. It'd be useless for him to now follow the jugger – something that would have been easy enough – and see what it did to Macsen, because he'd just be offering himself up as its next target.

Macsen had done what he'd needed to do. He'd left the book, and led the jugger away, and that was his final act. Laylaw closed the book, and wrapped it in the soft skin. That it had ended this way was sad. That it had ended at all was sad. But it was at an end, and in a way that meant that he didn't have to refuse Macsen help, and show himself up further.

He could even make up a story about how Macsen came to realise that he'd lost the book himself, and that he'd been wrong to blame Laylaw. He didn't even have to make anything up, though he suspected that no one would believe the true version of events. If he wanted that, he'd have to concoct something extraordinary, and he wasn't sure he had the imagination to do so.

It would be better to stick to the facts. If anyone asked how they'd found the book, he'd tell them plainly that it was a miracle, and he couldn't explain it, and leave it at that. That, at least, was the truth too. He couldn't explain it. Neither was he going to attempt to. Macsen had found the book, had left it for Laylaw, and now he was going to hand it to Hona Loy.

Laylaw walked back to his horse, and put the book into his saddlebag, and then checked that he'd put the book into his saddlebag, because to lose it twice would be ridiculous. Although, no one would ever know. He could just claim Macsen had never found it. But because he wanted to do right by Macsen, completing his final quest for him, he'd keep on checking throughout the journey.

There was Macsen's horse to bring back too. It was important to the tribe that they didn't lose it, so he tied a rope between his saddle and the bridle, and hopefully it'd be biddable enough that it would follow through the forest, across the river, and up into the hills without causing problems. He'd cut it loose if necessary, but he was returning without Macsen as it was: the least he could do was bring back his horse.

He could find his way back. Of course he could. Even if he always left the navigating to Macsen, he wasn't a complete idiot. Craig Low wasn't hard to find: over the ridge and down the hill into the valley, find and cross the ford, then strike uphill until he found the outflow from the lake. He'd have been spotted by then, and that would be that.

He remembered his fear, though, that the tribe would move on without him. In his dreams, they'd been forced to move by the visitors. Perhaps a coreship had headed towards the camp, which they'd then have to abandon, and quickly. Perhaps a tanker might threaten them. Most unpredictable of all, a spike. They were safe from a sphere, unless one had found its way into the lake. Which was unlikely, as they seemed to stick to the bigger rivers.

Once upon a time, there'd been bridges. The spheres seemed deliberately designed to destroy them, and enforce the division of the land represented by rivers. Little bridges over little rivers were apparently allowed, but all the big bridges, the ones made out of stone or concrete or steel were brought down very early on in the occupation. What did they do after that except patrol the same water course, up and down, making sure that no other bridges were built?

Ships, he supposed. There used to be ships, huge boats made of metal that plied the oceans, going from one continent to the next, moving things around, though for what purpose he was never quite certain. A sphere could take out a ship, holing it below the waterline and sinking it in short order. Again, they seemed to ignore the skin-covered coracles they sometimes used for fishing, in the same way they'd not demolish a tree felled over a river.

Those were his dreams. In his nightmares, the tribe had simply packed up and gone, and left him all alone, not so much banished as snubbed. He'd arrive back, and they would have gone. His heart would break, and then he'd wake up. If he was safe in the men's lodge, he'd lie awake and listen to the sounds of breathing, and slowly fall back to sleep. If he was out questing with Macsen, then that would be it for the night. He'd hear every twig snap and every bird call until dawn.

He looked behind him, and didn't see Macsen. He'd get used to it, in time. He checked his saddlebag again, and yes, the book was still there. There wasn't any point in hanging around. There was a jugger in the area, and he ought to put some distance between him and it, in case it had already killed Macsen and was aimlessly searching for its next target.

Laylaw mounted up and rode away. Macsen's horse did appear content to just follow along. He rode over the rise, then down the other side, making sure that he was always heading downhill. The sun was an intermittent companion, but as long as he kept it behind him, he knew he was heading in roughly the right direction.

At some point, he encountered the disturbed ground caused by the coreship, and rather than view it as a hazard, he took heart that he wasn't lost. He'd never done this before, been out in the wilderness on his own, let alone been responsible for two valuable horses. He walked them across one at a time, and tied them back up together when he was done.

He'd find the edge of the treeline soon, because beyond that was where they'd watched the coreship from. He realised that this wasn't particularly difficult: he knew what to look for, recognised the important waymarkers, remembered which order they had to come in. Why had he been scared of this? It didn't make any sense. It had been an irrational fear, and now exposed as such, it had lost its power over him.

The sky lightened, and he broke through into the water meadows down by the river. Finding the ford meant trailing along the bank until the shingle rose to the surface, and showed itself as threaded bands across the width of the water. He led the horses splashing through. The water was brown with peat from the uplands: where it was deep, it turned the river bed bronze, and in the shallows, golden.

Then he mounted up for the final leg of the journey. He could already see the crag that loomed over Craig Low, and the crease in the landscape that hid the route up to the lake, although he'd lose both features as he grew closer. But they were there, and he could find them. He'd be there by nightfall, or soon after. Once he was heading up, he wasn't going to get lost.

There was the outflow from the lake, tumbling down the hillside between the trees. Laylaw recognised it and nudged his horse in that direction. It grew gloomy, and then darker still as the sun settled down on the western horizon, below the long, low range of mountains. At some point, he'd encounter the watch. He walked beside the stream, keeping it on his right, just as Macsen had done yesterday, and always expected a call, a challenge, the sound of a horn.

It didn't come, and suddenly Laylaw was at the top, in the open space before the lake. The tents were gone, the temporary structures taken apart and laid down. The people had gone. The animals had gone. He felt his heart stop – just cease, mid-beat. Everything he'd dreaded most in the world had just come true. The tribe had left him behind.

"Laylaw?" And it started again, leaving him light-headed with relief. His hands were shaking, and his closed them tight around the reins of the lead horse. He couldn't see who it was who had spoken his name, but he knew her voice. He was afraid all over again, but for different, bitter-sweet reasons.

"Hona? Hona Loy?" He stood, trembling, as she emerged from the shadows and came towards him, her face pale and serious in the half-light. The tribe might have moved on, but she'd waited for him. Though, not him. She'd waited for Macsen. And now he had to tell her that he wasn't coming back. She might already have guessed, with there being two horses and only one man, but he'd still have to shape the words and say something.

She came and stood in front of him, her dark eyes counting one and two, two and one. That made it a little easier, he supposed. Hona Loy wasn't stupid. He took a deep breath to begin his explanation, but she turned away. "I'll light a fire. We can talk then," she said. There was already a small pile of kindling on the ground behind her, and she bent to strike it alight.

It lit cleanly and easily, and she placed larger pieces of wood around it, waiting for them to catch. When it was properly ablaze, she sat back on her haunches and waited for Laylaw to join her. He was still holding the horses, and hadn't dared move. Now he couldn't not. He took the horses up to the nearest grazing and tied them on long leashes, so they could roam more freely. He remembered to retrieve the book, which was thankfully there, and hadn't mysteriously disappeared.

He carried it back to the fire. Now was a better time to give it to her, rather than front of a crowd. Gone were all thoughts of seeing how she'd react to the death of Macsen, thoughts that, in the event, seemed less than worthy. Worthless, even. Macsen had gone. She could feel whatever she wanted: sorrow, despair, anger, indifference, resignation. Laylaw didn't know what he ought to be feeling himself, so who was he to dictate her emotions?

He sat down next to her and simply handed her the book with no preamble or ceremony. She hesitated for a moment, then took it from him. She held it, still wrapped up, against herself. Hugging it close. It wouldn't bring him back, but it might mean something of him transferred from the wrap and onto her.

"I'm sorry," he said. "There was a jugger. There was nothing either of us could do. It picked him, and not me. He…" His voice cracked, and he swallowed. "He went bravely. No pleading or begging. He cursed it, and then led it away, towards the rubble. The book – I don't know how he found it. A tanker had been through the clearing we'd used. But he found it all the same."

She placed the book in her lap, and pressed her hand on top of it. "Losing the book wasn't your fault, was it?" She glanced sideways at him. "There's only you and me. I won't tell anyone if it was, but I'm not wrong, am I? You gave the book to him, and somewhere between there and here, it disappeared."

Laylaw wondered what to say, then realised the truth was the only way forward. "It was as I said at the time: I put it in his saddlebag. I don't know how it came to be where he found it. Perhaps he… No. I'm not speaking ill of the dead. It was a miracle, and they don't happen that often, do they? It was lost, now it's found. Almost as if Macsen swapped places with it. He was found, and now he's lost."

He stared into the glowing heart of the fire. "I didn't want to go questing with him. I never wanted to go questing with him. Everyone expected me to go because I was his cousin, and I was too weak to ever say no. So I ended up, lonely and afraid, waiting for him, hating myself, and hating him. Every time he went, I told myself I'd never put myself through it again. Every time he came back, I'd be so relieved, I'd forget what it was like. This was going to be the last one. I finally told him I'd had enough. I wasn't going questing with him any more."

"One last quest," said Hona Loy. "One last quest. We had a coreship. We had just enough warning. We lost a couple of goats. A pig. We got most of the chickens back, even if we lost all the eggs. They can actually fly, even from all the way up there. It demolished the camp, caused a rock slide that sent a wave over the edge of the lake and through the middle of the tents. It was time to head towards the gathering anyway, so when it had gone, we packed up everything we could. They set off, and I said I'd stay behind and wait for you."

"You were waiting for Macsen, weren't you? Not me. If that's what you did, then that's what you did. There was nothing I could do. You can't reason with a jugger. You can't make it change its mind. It picked Macsen. There's no point in either of us wishing it hadn't. I'm not Macsen. I'm not anything like Macsen. But he's gone and I'm still here."

"You're right," she said. "You can't change anything. If Macsen hadn't lost the book, he wouldn't have had to go out again. Then, the jugger might have met us on the way to the gathering, and picked someone else. It might have picked me. It could have happened to any of us. It still can. That's the way it works."

Hona Loy unfolded the skin, and stroked the cover of the book. "This is beautiful," she said. She lifted the front board, and looked at the red endpapers. She turned the pages, one by one. At the beginning, some of the pages were blank. Others had only a few words, collected in small blocks. One had just two, right at the very top, in tiny, curly script. "For Judith. I wonder who Judith was?"

"The book's a couple of hundreds of years old. She'll be dead. The person who wrote this will be dead. Everyone involved with the book is dead." Laylaw frowned. "What does it matter? Some made it. Most didn't. We can't say that our ancestors were any better than anyone else. They just didn't die, that's all."

He looked up into the darkened sky, and Hona Loy turned a few more pages. He could hear the crisp rasp her fingers made on the ivory paper. She cleared her throat, angled the book towards the firelight and began to recite: "I once played the cowardly lion; a coward not only in script, whispered some who'd not cottoned on – seeing how feart I was of a playground leathering; of muddying my clothes on the pitch; of the opposite sex – the courage to weep could compensate. Bit of a cross to bear.

You had your crosses too, hard as nails and heavier.

They may mean you feel no Venus, but to me you're a bronze shield cast by Vulcan or a new earthenware goblet brimming with wine."

She closed the book gently, and wrapped it back up again. "They're not dead, Laylaw. They were, but now we get to hear their voices again. As long as we have stories, we'll never die."

"Like Macsen's? Is that what he was after? He wanted to live forever? Did he tell you that?" Laylaw listened to the crackling of the fire, and the sound of the wind blustering against the high crag. "I suppose it was the sort of thing he would say. I suppose in the end he gets his wish, too. We'll keep on telling his stories, but they won't get written down. So they'll change. They'll change and grow, and get bigger and wilder, and there'll be gods and monsters and every kind of adventure in them. We'll die, and the stories will go on without us. You can't change the words in a book, but storytellers aren't like books, are they?"

"No," said Hona Loy. She edged a little closer to Laylaw, and a little closer, until their knees were just touching. "Only you know the last story of Macsen. Only you know what happened. It's for you to tell now. You can tell it any way you want. You could say that his last words to you were for you to take up questing in his place, and that your last words to him were that you would."

Laylaw thought about it for a while. If Macsen's name was going to live on, what of Laylaw's? Was he going to be the eternal companion of the hero? Or was he going to write his own stories? He wasn't Macsen: he was right about that. But what if he didn't want to be Laylaw anymore? He – he could become Macsen. He could take Macsen's attributes, his skills, his daring. Assume his role.

And when Hona Loy called on him to take a quest, some time in the spring, she'd call him Macsen, and he'd answer as he always answered. Not with a question, but with an estimate of how many days it would take him. Macsen would ride out again, with a different Laylaw by his side. The stories would go on. "Those were his last words," he heard himself say. "Those were mine."

About the Author

Doctor Simon Morden is geologist, space scientist, award-winning science educator and winner of the 2011 Philip K Dick award. The author of twelve novels, as well as novellas and short stories, his writing blurs the edges of genre boundaries, and neither readers nor publishers can be exactly sure of what they're getting. He lurches from one act of utter hubris to another, and his personal motto is "How hard can it be?"

An adopted northerner, he lives in Gateshead and uses short vowels. His website is bookofmorden.co.uk, and you can follow his splenetic utterances on twitter by following @ComradeMorden.

NewCon Press Novellas Set 5: The Alien Among Us

Nomads – Dave Hutchinson

Are there really refugees from another time living among us? And, if so, what dreadful event are they fleeing from? When a high speed car chase leads Police Sergeant Frank Grant to Dronfield Farm, he finds himself the focus of unwanted attention from Internal Affairs and is confronted by questions he's not sure he ever wants to hear answered.

Morpho – Philip Palmer

When the corpse on the mortuary slab sits up and speaks to Hayley, asking for her help, she thinks she's losing her mind. If only it were that simple… Philip Palmer delivers a tense fast-paced tale of a secret society that governs our world from the shadows, of immortality at a terrible price and events that lead to the overthrow of social order.

The Man Who Would Be Kling – Adam Roberts

When two people ask the manager at Kabul Station to take them into the Afghanizone he refuses. What sane person wouldn't? Said to represent alien visitation, the zone is deadly. Nothing works there. Electrical items malfunction or simply blow up. The pair go in anyway, and the biggest surprise is when one of them walks out again. Nobody survives the zone, so how has she?

Macsen Against the Jugger – Simon Morden

Two centuries after the Earth fell to alien machines known as the Visitors, humanity survives in sparse nomadic tribes. Macsen is an adventurer, undertaking hazardous quests to please Hona Loy. Macsen never fails, but this time he is pitted against a deadly Jugger. Can he somehow survive, or will it fall to his faithful companion Laylaw to tell the tale of his noble death?

NewCon Press Novellas

Released in sets of four, each novella is an independent stand-alone story. Each set is linked by shared cover art, split between the books, providing separate covers that link to form a single image greater than the parts.

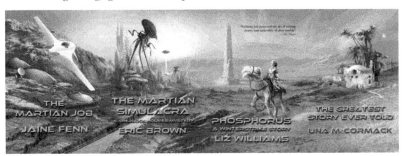

Set 1: Science Fiction
Novellas by Alastair Reynolds, Simon Morden, Anne Charnock, Neil Williamson.
Cover art by Chris Moore

Set 2: Dark Thrillers
Novellas by Simon Clark, Alison Littlewood, Sarah Lotz, Jay Caselberg.
Cover art by Vincent Sammy

Set 3: The Martian Quartet
Novellas by Jaine Fenn, Eric Brown, Liz Williams, Una McCormack.
Cover art by Jim Burns

Set 4: Strange Tales
Novellas by Gary Gibson, Adam Roberts, Ricardo Pinto, Hal Duncan.
Cover art by Ben Baldwin

Set 5: The Alien Among Us
Novellas by Dave Hutchinson, Philip Palmer, Adam Roberts, Simon Morden.
Cover art by Peter Hollinghurst

Each novella is available separately in paperback or as a limited numbered hardback edition, signed by the author. Each set is available as a strictly limited lettered slipcase set, containing all four of the books as signed dust-jacketed hardbacks and featuring the combined artwork as a wrap-around.

www.newconpress.co.uk

IMMANION PRESS
Purveyors of Speculative Fiction

www.immanion-press.com

Vivia by Tanith Lee

Tanith Lee was writing grimdark fantasy even before it was known as a genre. Gritty, savage and darkly erotic, *Vivia* is one of the author's darkest - and finest - works. Vivia, the neglected daughter of a vicious warlord, discovers strange, lightless caverns deep beneath her father's castle. Here she finds an entity she believes is a living god and, in her loneliness, seeks its favour. After war and disease devastate her father's lands, Vivia is taken captive by the hedonistic Prince Zulgaris and kept as his concubine. In this barbaric land, where life means very little, and the spectre of the plague haunts the alleys and markets of even the greatest city, circumstances can change very quickly. No life is safe, and treachery abounds. Perhaps, in such a brutal world, only remote pitiless creatures like Vivia can survive unscathed. But at what cost? ISBN: 978-1-907737-98-5 £12.99 $16.99

Songs to Earth and Sky edited by Storm Constantine

Six writers explore the eight seasonal festivals of the year, dreaming up new beliefs and customs, new myths, new dehara – the gods of Wraeththu. As different communities develop among Wraeththu, the androgynous race who have inherited a ravaged earth, so fresh legends spring up – or else ghosts from the inception of their kind come back to haunt them. From the silent, snow-heavy forests of Megalithican mountains, through the lush summer fields of Alba Sulh, into the hot, shimmering continent of Olathe, this book explores the Wheel of the Year, bringing its powerful spirits and landscapes to vivid life. Nine brand new tales, including a novella, a novelette and a short story from Storm herself, and stories from *Wendy Darling, Nerine Dorman, Suzanne Gabriel, Fiona Lane* and *E. S. Wynn*. ISBN 978-1-907737-84-8 £11.99 $15.50 pbk

TANITH LEE FROM IMMANION PRESS

We are committed to republishing Tanith Lee's long out of print or rare to find novels. The *Blood Opera Sequence* is Tanith's unique take on the vampire myth. If the Scarabae family are indeed vampires – and no one knows for sure – you'll find no others like them in literature or on film.

Dark Dance

After her mother's death, Rachaela is stalked by agents of the mysterious Scarabae family. Despite her instincts to keep away from the Scarabae, she ultimately relents and is taken to the rambling, isolated house near the sea, where they live in baroque seclusion. The fading splendour of the house closes around Rachaela like a stifling womb, and she's given no explanation for the ménage of bizarre oldsters, who are like creatures from an earlier age, and certainly not normal. Is there something supernatural to the Scarabae, or are they merely lost in delusion? ISBN 978-1-907737-85-5 pbk £12.99

Personal Darkness

The Scarabae, an unconventional and eccentric family, who might not be entirely human, have been forced to leave their reclusive home in a remote part of England. Some are dead at the hands of a child created through incest with the purpose of repopulating this ageing branch of the family. Rachaela trails listlessly with the survivors of the Scarabae. She is one of them but still can't feel that she is. The Scarabae relocate to London, and roost within a baroque old mansion. Here, they lick their wounds, but bizarrely appear to be growing younger and mysterious deaths begin to mount up in the city. ISBN 978-1-907737-86-2 pbk £12.99

Darkness I

Anna is no ordinary girl. Her parents and the other Scarabae don't know that another member of the family has become aware of her – the father of them all, the almost mythical Cain, who lives apart from the world in a frozen wasteland, where's he's constructed a bizarre reproduction of Ancient Egypt within a pyramid of ice. He wants not only Anna, but other children he believes are reincarnations of people from the past – the earliest times of the family. But what does he want them for? Soon, the kidnappings begin… ISBN 978-1-907737-95-4 pbk £12.99

www.immanion-press.com

CPSIA information can be obtained
at www.ICGtesting.com
Printed in the USA
LVHW112241080519
617103LV00005B/709/P